I0594360

# THE HOURGLASS MAP

Ryan **Collins**  Stuart **Kells**

The Hourglass Map
© Ryan Collins and Stuart Kells, 2020

THE LANE PRESS PTY LTD
PO Box 6038
South Yarra, Victoria, 3141, Australia
books@thelanepress.com.au

First published October 2020 by The Lane Press Pty Ltd

All rights reserved. Without limiting the rights under copyright reserved above, no part of this publication may be reproduced, stored in or introduced into a database and retrieval system or transmitted in any form or any means (electronic, mechanical, photocopying, recording or otherwise) without the prior written permission of both the owners of copyright and the above publisher.

The publisher and authors acknowledge the Traditional Custodians of the lands and waters throughout Australia and pay respect to the stories, traditions and ongoing living cultures of First Nations People.

Cover design by Naomi Creek

Written and produced in Australia

A catalogue record for this book is available form the National Library of Australia

ISBN: 9780648960904 (paperback)
ISBN: 9780648960911 (ebook)

# CONTENTS

# PROLOGUE

Ashburnham High.

Building B.

Room 8.

Mrs Crabbe's year eleven history class.

*I should be grateful to be here*, Will Page thinks. *Just need to keep up.*

Ashburnham is a university school. The professors of Sandstone University send their children here to learn the most important facts. The History of the World, and, even more essential, The Theory of Everything.

Sandstone is famous. It's the largest and most prestigious university in Port Philip, the capital of the Australian Republic, and it's home to a magnificent device. The Consistency Engine. An enormous, mechanical supercomputer. The unique, physical embodiment of the Theory. The source of the answers to all the important questions – of which, it is said, very few remain to be asked.

*I should be grateful to be here.*

Will is sitting right behind Todd Macdonald. The Vice Chancellor's son. The class bully. Will is shorter than most of the boys and many of the girls in his year level. He is a good four inches shorter than Todd and much less filled out.

Will feels scrawny in comparison. And he feels scrawnier still whenever he's with his older friend, Tim 'Loopy' Weston. Will and Loopy grew up together in Redcliffe, a country town two hundred miles inland. They'd once been inseparable. But then Will's family moved to Port Philip. After that, the pair saw each other only occasionally. Until two months ago, that is, when they had an awkward reunion. Will's old friend became Ashburnham's new cleaner.

Will would rather not be right behind Todd in class – or anywhere else. But the seats are allocated alphabetically. And there is no arguing, Will concedes, with the alphabet. Plus the ordering isn't all bad. It puts Will right near Todd's twin sister, Laura.

For forty-five minutes every Tuesday and forty-five minutes every Thursday, Will's gaze is drawn again and again to the fascinating profile of Laura's longish neck and squarish head. The intriguing contours of her shoulders. The patterns in her brown braided hair. The ridges and valleys of her smiling, velvety ears…

*I'm grateful to be here.*

Today, Todd catches him staring.

'Stop gawping,' he snarls.

Laura notices neither the staring nor the snarling. She is utterly focused on something in her open desk drawer. Will leans forward, cranes his shortish neck to see what it is. An old leather box braced by tight silver bands and decorated with a strange tangle of inlaid patterns.

In the instant before Laura lifts the object and holds it to her chest, Will catches sight of the box's red velvet lining. To get a better line of sight he leans further forward and to the left. And that means leaning closer to Todd, who catches Will looking a second time.

'Yippy scum!'

These words are never far from Todd's lips. Will knows exactly what they mean.

Will's mother, Dr Mary Page, had once worked at Sandstone. The Chancellery – the university's board of governors – forced her out because of her research on alternative histories. Unsound research, they'd said at the time.

Mary's dismissal didn't faze her. She persisted in her work, becoming the poster child for the Yippies: cranks and outcasts who believe in man-eating plants and shape shifters and other impossible creatures like minyips and bunyips. (A minyip is to a bunyip what an alpaca is to a llama, or a rock wallaby to a red kangaroo.) And then, during a disastrous expedition to the centre of Australia, she disappeared. Will was eleven years old when he vowed that, one day, he'd discover her fate.

Today he is almost seventeen, Mary's disappearance is still a mystery, and Will has had enough of Todd's insults. This time, he decides, he will make Laura's brother take it back.

As he stands to face the boy he feels a hard whack to the side of his head. Todd is fast and skilful but Will isn't entirely unprepared. In Redcliffe he'd learnt how to fight by sparring with Loopy. How to block. How to stay balanced. How to take a blow.

Now armed with that hard-won knowledge, Will dodges a second punch before delivering one of his own to the bully's chin. In a fury Todd grabs Will with both hands and pulls him to the floor. The boys tumble and roll, knocking over desks and sending pens and paper flying. In the commotion Laura is knocked from her seat and she, too, tumbles to the floor. As the boys wrestle, a strange, gourd-like artefact falls from the box in Laura's hands. Will catches a glimpse as it skitters across the floor. Flashes of blue and ochre and beige spin by on the object's smooth, glossy surface.

Mrs Crabbe pounces on the brawlers and shepherds them to the detention room. As he leaves the classroom, Will sees Laura reaching under the sideboard to retrieve the mysterious artefact. Its colours remind Will of the ancient maps he saw on the class fieldtrip to the Mandelbrot Museum.

Ignoring the uproar, Laura reverently replaces the object in its case and returns to her desk, where she traces her right index finger dreamily in a continuous figure-eight along the contours of the main symbol on the box.

$$\infty$$

Normally, Mr Oakeshott teaches home economics. Today, though, he's in charge of two boys in trouble.

Actually, just one boy. After only a few minutes in detention, Todd MacDonald strides to the front of the room and starts to talk his way out. Will caused the fight, he asserts, and the Vice Chancellor wouldn't want his son confined for long. Oakeshott gives in and lets Todd leave, but Will is stuck. Without cards to play or strings to pull, he steels himself for many hours of writing out passages from the history text.

The universe, though, has other plans. Soon Will hears a faint tapping. Looking over his right shoulder he sees something, behind the flimsy mesh that covers the wide vent in the skirting board. A pair of eyes. A nose. A broad and slightly unhinged grin. The unmistakable face of Loopy Weston.

Pretending not to notice, Will waits till it's safe. Oakeshott falls sleep and escapes into a dream about the ideal cheesecake. Will escapes, too, by climbing into the vent.

In his studies at Ashburnham he always feels two steps behind. But in the maze of tunnels and viaducts that thread beneath the high school and the neighbouring university, his mind is always two turns ahead.

The heavy door to Cromwell's Cloister: will it be unlocked, or must he go the long way round, through the undercroft and via the trapdoor beside the supply dock? The hatchways below the stage in the Great Hall: will they be open, and will anyone be watching? And will the deepest tunnels be navigable, or still flooded after the late-autumn rains?

Generations of Ashburnham's pupils have assembled a rich body of lore – a kind of urban bushcraft – about where each tunnel goes, how best to thwart the gates, and the right times of day at which to pass unseen through courtyards, book-stacks, loading bays and kitchens.

Will knows the underground network better than he knows Mandelbrot's Complete Periodic Table, which all the school's students are forced to memorise. Soon after Loopy arrived at Ashburnham, Will inducted him into the secret subterranean lore. Loopy was soon exploring the tunnels as often as he could. He is fast becoming another expert.

Today, he leads Will through the narrow and twisting passageways. Along the aisles and through the vaults below the university library. Past alcoves and niches and traps. Down timeworn slides. Up creaking ladders.

Will matches his friend's speedy pace. At well over six feet tall, Loopy is often punished by squat archways and low-slung girders. Whenever he turns his sinewy frame sideways, to squeeze past this pipe or that barrier, Will catches glimpses of the tunnels ahead.

Those tunnels connect the basements and sub-basements of buildings on and near the main campus. Some are freshly built but most date from when the university was first founded, constructed for purposes long since forgotten. Something to do with heating, the bush-lore said. Or maybe arrowroot. Or gunpowder.

Whatever their original purpose, the secret ways below

Sandstone are now the natural habitat of Will Page and Loopy Weston.

On this day, Loopy has a gift to share with his younger friend. He hasn't told Will exactly what it is – only that it involves a stomach-churning spectacle.

'You're gunna love it,' Loopy says, leading the way to the narrow crawlspace that abuts the dissecting lab below the Department of Medicine and Surgery.

Lying flat, the friends peer through a high grille. They can see an instructor and eight med students standing in a loose circle around a stainless-steel demonstration table.

The instructor is tall and serious. She wears a white coat. Her students wear green scrubs. Lit up by halogens, the instructor lifts a cloth from a metal tray.

'Today's lesson,' she declares, 'is brain anatomy'.

'Toldya,' says Loopy.

Will elbows him in the side of his ribs.

'Quiet,' Will whispers.

On the metal tray a human brain lies exposed. Its convoluted surface, mottled yellow-brown and purple, is slimy and naked in the theatre lights. The secret observers stare, gobsmacked, while the medical students close in round the table.

The instructor picks up the brain, weighs it, then begins to describe its folded structure, her voice refracting off white tiles and stainless steel.

'These are the cerebellar hemispheres on the inferior aspect of the occipital lobes of the cerebrum, separated by the *tentorium cerebelli*. The hemispheres have superior and inferior surfaces. Between these you can see a fissure.'

The instructor pauses and flexes the brain to display its features more clearly. The opened brain reminds Will of an origami salt cellar.

'This is the horizontal fissure. On the superior surface, here, is the primary fissure. It separates the anterior lobe from the middle lobe.'

The instructor pauses again, then probes the deep horizontal cleft with a latex-gloved finger.

'This is the superior vermis of the cerebellum. And this . . .'

She turns the brain, bends it in her hands, splits it in two.

'This . . . is the interior.'

Will nearly loses his breakfast.

He has a silent understanding of why he is here. The anatomical spectacle is a well-meant gift from Loopy – a way for the old friends to share a secret experience. But it is also an unspoken challenge, a message of competition from someone who has always been an outsider and is one even more so now, thanks to his new, unglamorous role at Ashburnham.

As the dissection continues, Will watches for as long as he can without seeming weak. And without puking. At the end of the show, his face is as green as the med students' scrubs. His mind ponders images he'd rather forget.

Will and Loopy commando down a steep ladder that leads to the north-south service tunnel. The ladder seems to be held together by nothing more than rust, and perhaps the memory of having once been more sturdy.

No one in the dissecting lab hears the eavesdroppers leave. Any noise they make is damped by the low purr of exhaust fans, and by the deep, resonant hum of the Consistency Engine.

Will looks at his watch.

'I better head back,' he says. 'Old Oakeshott'll wake up soon.'

Loopy nods. As though steeling himself, he laces his fingers together, reaches forward and rounds his back until Will hears the vertebrae pop.

'I'm ready,' he says. 'Let's go.'

Again the pair advance along tunnels lit by flickering lights and lined with clanking pipes and bulging valves.

Every now and then a locked wire gate blocks their path. The trespassers make short work of these barriers, squeezing over and around them like ferrets.

Narrow, hot and grimy, the Chaffey passageway is lined with ancient-looking bricks. It runs beneath the main corridor of the admin wing of the university, where the senior academics have their offices. The Vice Chancellor occupies the biggest of them all, its walls decorated with portraits of Copernicus, Galileo, Edison and other Heroes of the Republic.

As Will and Loopy pass below that very office, they hear through a bronzed vent the voice of the VC himself.

Will is first to stop and listen. He knows, just as Loopy does, how dangerous it is for anyone, pupil or staff, to interfere with Chancellery business. The highest ranking men and women in the university also rank high in the government, and the military. But the two truants are drunk on the feeling of stolen freedom, and still shell-shocked by the gruesome dissection.

Climbing a cluster of pipes and ducts and cables, they peek into Macdonald's room.

∞

Will counts three men inside. He can see their boots and trousers, and he can tell one of the men is not a professor. The odd man out wears the uniform of a Republican army officer. The other two men are the VC, Professor Oliver Macdonald, and his right hand, Hector Mallory, the Bursar of Sandstone.

Will and Loopy know Macdonald's and Mallory's voices. Both men spoke at the opening of the school year at Ashburnham, and Macdonald is a celebrity on campus. His jutting jaw and booming orations make famous appearances in Midwinter debates and at formal openings and investitures and other ceremonies.

Mallory, too, is a celebrity of sorts. Every student knows that the Bursar's face bears a striking resemblance to the weathered, glowering gargoyle who oversees the gloomy north-west corner of the Cloister.

Gathered around the smaller of two mahogany tables, the men pass among themselves a set of photographs. Catching the words 'desert' and 'drones', Will inches closer so he can better see and hear.

Peering through the grille, he glimpses one of the enlarged images, a double exposure. It reminds him of a book he once saw in his father's personal library. The book told the story of the Cottingley Fairies, an early photographic hoax.

The VC fixes his attention on the photograph with the double image. The picture shows a featureless red desert – plus a shadowy image of a little girl. Her face is pale and freckled, her electric red hair cut precisely in a short bob. She wears a neat summer dress and, in her hair, yellow flowers. A thousand miles from any township or station or homestead, the girl is happily eating an ice-cream cone.

'What am I looking at?' Macdonald says testily.

The officer answers.

'We monitor the unpopulated inland, sir. With pilotless drones. The drones carry cameras and our tech department processes the images. They always come back blank. Nothing but sand and gravel. Except last week, sir, when the techoes tried a new emulsion. "Bugpowder Dust" they call it. Distilled from nutmeg. Kills weevils stone cold. Has other effects, too. Unpredictable effects. On the mind. Pervasive feeling of relaxation. Confusion, too. And sometimes blind panic. Situation's under control, sir.'

The VC and his deputy are suddenly concerned about the

residue of ginger-coloured dust that has accumulated on the images and now covers their fingers, palms and cuffs.

'Print a clean set,' the VC directs, 'then bring them to me immediately.'

The officer salutes and leaves.

'We also need to discuss Professor John Page,' Mallory says.

'The problem child of the physics department.'

'His latest work is especially unorthodox. Could become a risk.'

'Time for him to go.'

Mallory thinks about this for a moment, then asks in a hushed tone, 'Do we need to do more than dismiss him?'

The men exchange knowing glances.

'Let's keep Smith on the leash for now,' Macdonald says. 'He has an interest in the family, on account of his brother, and Dr Mary Page.'

Will can't contain himself. At the mention of his mother he lets out a gasp.

Turning and dropping in one lightning movement, the VC and the Bursar see the two faces behind the mesh. Neither man speaks but Macdonald makes a gesture whose meaning is clear. Mallory leaves the office to give the order: the university's security guards are to catch the spies in the tunnels.

Delirious with fear, Will and Loopy monkey down the pipes and flee in a direction that takes them to the most dangerous part of the underground maze.

Racing along a narrow tunnel that branches off the Chaffey passage, the pair turn a sharp corner into a little-used part of the network. Suspended cobwebs, heavy with dust and frass, droop like bunting across the tunnel. The pair push their way through and come upon a thick oak door, which they shove with all their strength.

'Put your shoulder into it!' Loopy urges.

The door opens to a crypt-like chamber. A long, steep flight of stone steps cuts the chamber in half. The stairs rise twenty feet before ending at a sheer wall of stone blocks.

The chamber and staircase seem to have been built centuries ago for some sort of ceremonial purpose. Strange symbols cover the walls and the floor and even the stairs. Unable to decipher the symbols, Will thinks they must be characters from a forbidden language.

'Dead end,' says Loopy, the adrenaline and danger audible in his voice.

Warily, Will climbs the stairs and approaches the wall. The ancient markings and mysterious surroundings make him feel as though he is taking part in some kind of secret ritual.

At the top of the staircase he runs his hands over the smooth stone blocks, feeling for cracks and crevices. One block stands slightly proud of the surface. Pressing it with both hands, he hears a satisfying click and sees a section of blocks swing away, creating an opening about two feet high.

Will pokes his head through the opening, then decides to chance his luck. Loopy bounds up the stairs and follows his friend through the secret door.

Finding themselves behind heavy red drapes, the pair search for a gap in the fabric. When they find one, they peek out into the enormous domed hall. The Chamber of Logic. The home of the Consistency Engine.

Light shines through stained-glass windows, refracting into disco-ball colours that play mischievously across the slate-paved floor. A huge machine, two storeys high and twenty metres wide, dominates the centre of the hall. A slow-motion hurricane in brass. The marvel of the world.

Capable of an infinite variety of computational tasks, the Engine can transform itself into an infinite variety of shapes. The machine's appearance at any given moment is said to reflect the main subject of its thoughts. Right now, it is shaped like a giant, golden orrery – a faithful model of the solar system.

Slowly the Engine turns on its central axis. Intricately sculpted planets advance along elegant elliptical orbits in an accurate clockwork orchestration replete with Sun, planets, moons and tilted rings. In the machine's understorey, cogs and gyroscopes buzz and whirr. Lower still, the strong stone floor hums and tremors under its burden.

Decades before, a team of designers and metalsmiths had worked in secret to build the Engine in a unique and mysterious way. They'd used a strange kind of fractal engineering, remarkable for its careful workmanship and intricate, repeating patterns.

For the scientists and moneymen who now run the university – and the Republic – the Engine serves as their central computer. It stores all the world's knowledge, purging it of contradictions. The Engine gives Australia's leaders the consistency they crave. (In fact they love it so much, they've assigned it a capital letter and put the principle of Consistency at the centre of science and government.)

Though all the world's citizens know of the Engine, few have actually seen it. The chamber is closed to all but the Chancellery and the Republic's uppermost guilds. Only members of the Chancellery may ask the Engine questions. Every three years, those members choose from among their number a Keeper of the Engine – a post of great prestige.

Transfixed by the whirling machine, Will steps forward from the curtains for a closer look. As he stares at the marvellous hurling globes, he is unaware of the presence of a stranger. Unaware, that is, until a strong hand clamps down hard on his shoulder.

'What are you doing here, boy?'

Something in the man's voice is chilling.

The stranger wears the sombre, charcoal-coloured business-suit of the Actuaries, the Republic's guild of stealthy assassins. His grey-blue eyes search Will's face minutely, memorising every detail.

'Speak up.'

'The door was unlocked,' Will says feebly.

'You've made a mistake, boy. Novices may not enter this chamber.'

Using some kind of Eastern pressure-point technique, the man grips Will's upper arm just below his left shoulder.

Fear pulses through the truant as he fumbles about for a plausible story, a plausible lie. He can't think of one.

'I . . . I just wanted to see the machine.'

The man's grip tightens, his fingers probing for tendons and ligaments and subchondral bone.

'What's your name, boy?'

After this, everything moves quickly.

Loopy is nabbed, too. The trespassers are separately interrogated. In short order Will is expelled – the very day his father, Professor John Page, is abruptly relieved of his duties in the physics department. Unsure of Loopy's fate, Will assumes that he, too, has been fired.

Times like this, Will really misses his mother.

∞

The Republican army sends more reconnaissance drones to take new photos at the exact coordinates where the little girl had apparently eaten her ice-cream. The techos don't believe the first image is real. They're sure it's some kind of glitch.

When the new negatives come back, the technicians process them with the old emulsion rather than the Bugpowder Dust. Their suspicion is right. The new images show nothing but the usual, featureless terrain.

The VC, though, is puzzled by the first strange picture. He takes it, along with the new ones, to the Chamber of Logic. He will ask a question of the Engine.

A chemical engineer by training, Oliver Macdonald had once been the Engine's Keeper. Certainly it is an exalted post, but also a dangerous one. A stint of service in that role can only end in one of two ways. Promotion, or termination.

Macdonald was a deft and sensitive Keeper. Promotion followed for him. Today, as he walks from his impressive office to the equally impressive Chamber, he recalls his Keeper work: how he made thousands of secret adjustments to the troublesome Engine, to smooth its operations and refine its computation of reality.

Publicly, the Engine needs no adjustment. The official role of the Keeper is only to tend the machine and make sure it is cleaned and lubricated. In practice, though, the Keeper is continually tuning it – because the world is not a perfect sphere, the year is not exactly three hundred and sixty-five days, the speed of light is not exactly constant, and because there are still cracks in the Theory of Everything, cracks the Keeper must paper over.

The VC now knows the Engine intimately. He even regards it as having its own personality, though he only ever communicates with it in a highly formal manner through the purpose-built keyboard and screen that replaced the original clunky key-punch and card-sorter interface.

Now, asking the question about the photographs, he adopts the respectful language he always uses when entering data into the enormous machine.

'An irregular photo, dear Engine, from the interior. It might represent an inconsistency. I would welcome your wise advice.'

Words appear on the screen. The Engine's gruff, automatic acknowledgement.

*I'll think about it. Get back to you.*

# PART I

---

## THE JOURNEY TO THE INTERIOR

# 1

## REDCLIFFE

MORE THAN ONCE IN the capital city, Will Page had caught himself longing for the quiet simplicity of rural Redcliffe. Now, though, his return to his hometown is a rude shock. Everything is familiar yet utterly alien. The smell of bitumen and ozone replaces for him the papery smell of academic labour. In place of the towering office buildings, the longest shadows are cast by the Masonic Hall and the Settler's Arms Hotel. And now he hears the hubbub flow of the river instead of the steady thrum of the Consistency Engine.

Redcliffe for its part has hardly changed since the Page family left. Stray dogs still prowl the main street. Magpies still bother currawongs and wattlebirds outside Jan's Cafe. Cat Purren is still the town mechanic, Bob Evans the friendly shopkeeper, Mr Beveridge the chief busybody and prize-winning producer of cakes and azaleas. In front of each house each week, different coloured wheelie-bins continue to gather, making secret plans.

Not so long ago, the people of Redcliffe had regarded Will and his father as two of their own. When Mary chased a delusion and failed to return, the townsfolk gossiped, but there was sympathy in the gossip. Now, there is even more whispering behind closed doors. But instead of sympathy there is a new realisation, a new fatalism. The Page family is cursed. Clever, yes. But cursed.

Will senses this shift in the judgement of his neighbours. And perhaps they are right, he thinks, as he rides his bike past picket fences and deep bluestone kerbs before arriving at the front yard of the small turn-of-the-century cottage he shares with his father.

'Picked up some bread and milk,' he calls out as he walks through the front door.

His father sits silently at the kitchen table. He is holding a watch that has an oversized face and a thick leather band. He stares as the hands tick inexorably.

'Always forward, never back,' John Page says, maybe to Will, maybe to himself, possibly to no one at all.

'Got you another tin of peaches, too,' Will says. 'I know how much you've taken to them.' He puts a large tin in the cupboard, where there are already ten more just like it. In the corner of the kitchen, twelve empty cans stand haphazardly in a tower that somehow defies both gravity and the recycling.

Since leaving Sandstone and Ashburnham, the Pages have fallen into something of a routine. Will plans to complete his schooling at the local secondary college. John has taken up tinkering as a way to get by.

But in a town the size of Redcliffe there are only so many broken radios to fix. And only so many neighbours willing to open their doors to the man that John Page has become.

Though he was never particularly fastidious in his daily routine, there are now signs of John letting himself go. The day he left Sandstone he stopped shaving. And he definitely hasn't had a haircut since then, either. But he isn't dirty. Daily showers – sometimes twice daily – see to that. Will notices for the first time that his father smells faintly of iodine and citrus. It's an old-man smell.

If John heard Will's announcement about the peaches, he doesn't respond. Will thinks better of leaving them with the growing collection in the cupboard. He retrieves them, grabs the can-opener from the second top drawer and heads out through the fly-mesh door and into the backyard.

An old wooden ladder leans against the rear of the house. Will climbs it and picks his way across the corrugated zinc sheets to the apex of the roof. Once there, he punctures the peach-tin and takes a long swig of the sickly syrup. The metallic tang of the tin itself lingers long after the peach-flavoured sweetness has left.

Looking out across the neighbourhood's rooftops, Will notices the one that belongs to the milkbar. At this time of day, Mr Fiorini will be putting out the empty crates for collection. Mrs Fiorini will be keeping her eyes on the local kids, whose hands always seem to hover too long between their pockets and the tubs of loose confectionery in front of the counter.

Will's earliest memory is of riding his father's shoulders to that milkbar, with the promise of freckles and choc buds and ice-cream and sherbet sticks. Three steps ahead, Will's mother walks in the same memory. She talks thoughtfully about history and reality and the shape of things to come. Every now and then she turns to face the two men in her life, even walking backwards for a stretch.

Each time she turns, her face is slightly different. Perhaps it's a trick of the light. Maybe there are subtle changes in how she holds her expressive face. Or maybe, Will thinks, it's just an effect of how, day by day, his memory of her grows more distant, exaggerated, fractured.

Will closes his eyes on his rooftop perch and indulges further in the memory. In his mind's eye he can see his father's face – but that must be a false memory given his shoulder-based vantage point.

His father smiles generously as he pokes and prods at his mother's theories. The objections he raises are good-natured but laser-sharp. At first, Mary attempts a playful rebuttal. And then there is something else.

By the time the family has reached the corner before the milkbar, his mother's face is darker, her brow furrowed, her finger pointing. Will can't remember all of what Mary said, but he recalls snatches and phrases. 'Ideologically blinkered.' 'Academically ossified.' 'Methodologically bankrupt.' Impossible vocabulary for a toddler to digest. Maybe these, too, are false recollections.

John is fully capable of holding his own. Rising to the debate, he fires back with critiques of his own. Mary's position is unempirical, morally hazardous and Consistency-proof.

Will opens his eyes and he is back on the roof, back in the present. Pushing two fingers into the can, he pulls out a quarter peach just as he hears the back-door fly off its hinges. Craning his head forward, he sees John dash to the clothesline trailing a string tied with eight empty peach-tins.

Hanging the tins from a tubular arm of the clothesline, John grabs one of the four metal corners and spins the hoist as hard as he can. Counting six fast rotations, he catches the apparatus, brings it to a dead stop and moves the watch from one peach-tin to another. Then he spins the clothesline again and again, checking the timepiece after every batch of circumnavigations.

Will looks on in stunned fascination as his father becomes more and more animated. Then the animation reaches a crescendo and the former professor grabs hold of a crossbar and pulls himself up to hang precipitously with his knees tucked into his chest. Riding around and around, he stops only when gravity, exhaustion and metal-fatigue dictate that he must.

*'Academically ossified' indeed.*

Will takes a bite of peach and looks out across the rooftops once more. He misses the days when peaches were peaches and family discussions were exercises in scientific and philosophical brinkmanship.

2

———

## A LACK OF CONSISTENCY

THE PEACH-TIN EXPERIMENT is not the end of John Page's erratic behaviour. In fact, it's more of a beginning. He takes to loitering outside the main-street shops, stepping in and out of the shadows as if playing crocodiles or in deep conversation with himself. In the emporium, he turns all the jam jars upside down, until Mr Evans shoos him away.

The living areas of the Page household begin to fill with unwashed clothes, and with in-between garments that are too clean to wash but not clean enough to put away. For his part, Will tries to keep up the *momentum* of a normal life even if the *appearance* of one seems out of reach most days. To Will, his father was always a protector, a prodder, a mentor. Now, he is a cat to be herded, a discordant note, a problem to be solved.

Given what had happened at Sandstone, and what is now happening at Redcliffe, Will thinks it best for father and son to keep their heads down. At least for a while. John, though, refuses to curl into a ball. Instead he makes plans for a major event. A spectacular presentation to the eminent people of Redcliffe. A public lecture on his favourite metaphysical theories.

He advertises the lecture at the local library. *Masonic Hall. Evening discussion. Theoretical Physics. John Page.*

The night of the lecture arrives and Will sits quietly at a table in the Page living room while his father rushes about having forgotten this or remembered that. This is a special occasion and the former professor is wearing his academic robes and his plush Tudor bonnet.

During John's time at Sandstone, a fine red tassel was the regulation decoration for this bonnet. Now, though, there is another decoration. In place of the tassel, he has looped the leather band of a watch so that the face hangs just above his left temple.

*Can't be a mad scientist without a crazy hat,* Will thinks, then quickly admonishes himself. *Now is a time for sympathy, not jokes at the old man's expense.*

Will's eyes scan the living room before settling on a framed photo. A studio portrait of his mother. One of his most prized possessions.

He wants to barrage his father with questions but only one comes out. The one that has been on his mind for half a decade.

'Will we ever see her again?'

John stops fussing and stares, suddenly in a daze. Then he refocuses, apparently with great strain. Shrugs his shoulders. Looks at the floor.

'I don't know.'

'If she's alive, why'd she never come back?'

'She was always very . . . adventurous,' John says, momentarily losing his facility with words. 'Always questioning, always challenging. Science. The Theory. People in authority. But I challenged her, too. Told her she was wrong in so many of her beliefs. Mostly she was patient with me. But she tired of hearing my objections. We were at odds on so many things, and I couldn't help but tell her. In hindsight that was a mistake. You can't build a marriage on foundations like that.

Silence can destroy relationships, but it can also save them. At the time, I thought I was doing my best to make things work. Wounded me, her leaving.'

He pulls out a bentwood chair and sits down opposite Will at the table. Then he reaches across and takes hold of his son's hands.

'I was powerless to stop her. And after she went missing I was too hurt to speak much about it. But I'm sorry I didn't say more.'

Seeing the effort his father has made to collect his thoughts, Will is grateful for this moment of familiarity and disclosure, even if it makes him desperate for more answers.

'The expedition to the interior was a special kind of madness,' John continues. 'But she had to go through with it.'

Will thinks back to his last day at Sandstone, to the conversation he and Loopy had overheard about an ice-cream-eating girl in the interior and the impossibility of finding anything there besides a barren wasteland. The Vice Chancellor had mentioned Mary Page. What could that have meant?

'Why'd you stop looking for her?' Will asks. The question drops like a blunt instrument.

John looks down, clearly sensing the criticism in the question – a criticism that has weighed on his son's mind and their relationship.

John makes a strong defence. He'd searched thoroughly, he says, with the best trackers. Had even asked the Republic for help. All his savings went towards funding the search. He hadn't given up at the time. Hasn't given up even now. He'd do anything, he says, to find her.

*Anything?* Will wonders. *Does that include calling off tonight's lecture and focusing on something less public and more productive?*

John stands, pushes back his chair and rushes from the

room. As swiftly as it arrived, the brief interlude of sanity and clarity is over.

From the front door John calls back in his best White Rabbit voice.

'Mustn't be late!'

Reluctantly, Will follows.

He has inherited his mother's uncanny ability to read John's face. He can always tell when his father is uncomfortable, and when he isn't completely open about things. This time, Will knows his father has held something important back. He can't fix exactly on the nature of the falsehood, or its size, but he knows his father is lying.

∞

John had told the truth about searching thoroughly. In the aftermath of Mary's disappearance, the professor searched beyond the points of exhaustion and despair. But he hadn't told the whole truth about that terrible episode. John's search was more conclusive than he let on.

He'd found traces of the expedition: ruined equipment, butchered livestock, signs of violence and of the party breaking up. In multiple directions he'd followed footprints, some of which ended at sun-dried bodies. Mary's tracks ended at nothing at all.

Apart from these unhappy facts, John Page conceals from his son yet another truth. A much deeper one. Or a more profound lie.

∞

The doorway to the Masonic Hall is wide open. The yellow light spills out across the plaza in front, attracting a thousand moths and other flying insects with the false promise of an impossible sun. Most of the town's residents have turned out, too. They've come to see the astonishing spectacle of John Page explaining string theory, quantum entanglement, strange attraction, and the newest developments in theoretical physics.

John mounts the stage, clears his throat, welcomes the audience and begins with his favourite story. The tale of the 'double slit experiment' and the remarkable, paradoxical nature of light.

He tells of how, according to one longstanding scientific tradition, the smallest pieces of light were thought to be particles: tiny objects that travelled through space. And he explains the competing view, long held by many other scientists, that light was actually a wave: an immaterial pulse that moved through the fabric of space and time like waves in water.

Each backed by their own evidence, the opposing scientific camps had dug in long ago behind their own theories, which were utterly inconsistent. Light was either a particle or a wave. One of the camps had to be wrong. The purpose of the double slit experiment was to solve the impasse once and for all.

John tells of how a pair of scientists, one from each camp, had shone light through two narrow slits. In no time at all, sensors detected light particles – called photons – passing through the slits and hitting a photographic plate. Light, it seemed, did indeed consist of particles. The charismatic chief scientist from the particle camp couldn't contain himself. He leapt and whooped in triumph and relief.

But the experiment wasn't over. The shining light also left behind an unmistakable pattern on the plate. When the assembled scientists scrutinised it, they saw an interference pattern, just like the ones that waves make in water. Based on this evidence, which was incontrovertible, light just had to be a wave. Cheering and woo-hooing also came from the equally charismatic physicists in the wave camp.

The experiment caused a sensation. Its results became a pillar of modern physics, a key ingredient of the Theory of Everything and a mind-bending challenge to common sense. Both sets of scientists were right. Light had a strange dual character. Simultaneously, it behaved both as particles and as waves. Little bits of light were mysteriously connected.

This extraordinary result led the now reconciled physicists to experiment in a similar way with other phenomena. The scientists found something even more astounding. All sorts of objects displayed the same dual, wave–particle character. Electrons, neutrinos, quarks. Even larger objects like aeroplanes and people.

In Redcliffe's Masonic Hall, no one has ever spoken of such matters. *What utter nonsense*, some of the townsfolk think. *Sounds like heresy*, others mumble. *Surely this can't be consistent with the Theory*. On one point, though, there is near universal agreement. John Page has well and truly lost his marbles.

But how hard can it really be to convince the townsfolk that John has gone insane? Many already doubted his life story. Who among them actually believed a local boy could get as far as Sandstone University? Mr Beveridge was unimpressed even before the former professor began to speak.

'Knew he'd be back,' Will heard him say. 'Family tree is all madmen and bolters.'

Those words seem remarkably prophetic when, the day after his lecture, John Page disappears.

# 3

## GUARDIANS AND ANGELS

THE LEADERS of Sandstone and Ashburnham appreciated the neat symmetry of John Page being dismissed and Will Page being expelled on the same day. The expulsion, though, was unnecessary. Will would've left the school regardless, once his father left the science faculty. But the Chancellery in particular had relished the two-for-one opportunity to add another black mark to the official file of the Page family.

That feeling of satisfaction, though, doesn't last long. The Republic despises one thing above anything else – more than inconsistency and contradiction, more than speculation, and certainly more than uncertainty. The Republic abhors loose ends.

One month after putting the anomaly of the girl and her ice-cream to the Engine, the VC summons the university's head Actuary to his office. He has a task for him, an end that needs trimming. Few words are exchanged. There is little that goes on within the Republic that escapes the gaze of the Actuaries. Alan Smith knows his objective. He will set out immediately.

Returning to his austere quarters, he swaps his uniform

for corduroy slacks, a blue checked shirt and a brown cardigan. Simple, efficient, practical.

Ordinary.

Members of the Actuaries are selected in childhood for their ruthlessness – and their ordinariness. Dull-looking assassins can blend in. Witnesses at crime-scenes often discount them, or forget them altogether. The best Actuaries are like shadows. Or ghosts.

After their selection, Actuary novices enter an arduous program of physical and mental training. The training melds the gruelling methods of Chinese monasteries with the equally harsh strictures of chartered accountancy. It ensures that every Actuary has no personal quirks or aspirations or beliefs.

Nor any illusions. The assassins are trained to avoid the lies that people tell themselves. Instead, they must rely only on the real, sensory evidence that assists with their complete commitment to carrying out their deadly missions.

They see the world as it is.

In keeping with his appearance and a lifetime of training, Smith uses extremely ordinary methods to kill his targets. His most perfect murder, he remembers proudly, was spectacularly unremarkable. Local police discovered the body at an unexceptional time of day, lying prone on a front porch. The flowerpot that smashed the victim's skull was ordinary terracotta. The wound it inflicted was not exceptionally large. Nor was the pool of blood. Nothing out of the ordinary was seen or heard at the time of the murder.

Had eyewitnesses seen the killer, they would've described him as being unobtrusively dressed, of average height and weight, with a plain complexion, nondescript eyes and hair, and, in fact, possessing no distinguishing features of any kind at all.

Smith's hapless victim was a lime digger who'd recently found a mysterious set of very old keys.

In Redcliffe, John Page has vanished and Will Page's world should be falling apart. For one thing, he idolises his father. For another, he's been here before.

Abandoned, possibly orphaned, he experiences a second estrangement, one that brings back terrible memories of the loss of his mother.

This time, though, things are different. His most intense feeling is sadness, but that feeling, he thinks guiltily, is tinged with a sense of relief.

Redcliffe's local police and emergency volunteers soon wrap up their fruitless search for the missing former professor. Will packs a suitcase – unwashed clothes, his favourite books, his most cherished photographs – and goes to live in the old and rambling house of his father's old and rambling uncle.

Unmarried and with no children of his own, Maximillian Bunt has filled his house with antique furniture, old paintings, older books, a marvellous Wunderkammer, and a world-class collection of porcelain. In his vast greenhouses he propagates a unique selection of exotic flowers and herbs. In his kitchen, he bakes tea-cakes and pound-cakes that rival Mr Beveridge's prize-winners.

Throughout his collecting career, Max has amassed a large network of fellow aficionados. He maintains an active and friendly correspondence with distant enthusiasts of ceramics and horticulture, all of whom promise to call on him one day, if ever they happen to be in the neighbourhood.

In the meantime there are other visitors. The Ministry for Social Services assigns a pair of case officers to monitor the welfare of sixteen-year-old William Page. He first meets the officers when they appear on Uncle Max's doorstep.

One of them is an intimidating, fair-haired, six-foot-tall enforcer. Here to make sure everyone follows the rules. The other, a social worker, is shorter but no less official-looking. Will can tell immediately that she is a member of the anonymous class of recent migrants who do the bidding and legwork of the Republic.

Though her hair conforms precisely with the Ministry's mandated style, and though her clinically white dress exemplifies the official uniform of her profession, she wears on her right wrist a simple, solid-gold bracelet that is certainly not an authorised item. A family heirloom, she will tell whoever asks. A gift from her mother.

During the officers' first visit, while her sterner colleague is explaining some very official requirements to Uncle Max over a pot of tea, the junior officer, a student on placement, gives Will a very unofficial wink. An exhilarating, quickening wink.

Will thrills at this surprising but welcome message from the most delightful person he has ever seen. Even more delightful – can it be true? – than Laura Macdonald.

∞

Around social workers and other representatives of the Republic, Maximillian Bunt is always careful. With good reason: he harbours many of the old ways and much of the old wisdom that the Theory has officially superseded and that the authorities have officially banned.

He knows, for example, how to marshal the mysterious forces of hexes and mozzes and fate and luck. And he knows a great deal about angels and the bible. That book, he says to people he can trust, is a collection of beautiful stories, full of contradictions. And unlike the Republic, he relishes contradictions.

But Max is not all about rebellion. Though he breaks some of the Republic's regulations, he adheres rigidly to his own domestic rules. Will, too, is expected to follow them –

to the letter. No hats on beds. No pentagrams. No tall ladders. Shoes are to be lined up properly, with the left on the left and the right on the right. It is bad luck to pour tea from a pot that someone else has already poured. Worse still to leave the lid off – that means a stranger will pay a visit.

If, by accident, Will ever puts a jumper on inside out, Max says he has to wear it that way for the rest of the day, until the time comes when he would normally take it off. There are no umbrellas up indoors, of course, and when Max cuts a loaf of bread, he always looks inside for holes. A hole in the loaf, he says, is a portent that someone will die. And the bread never lies.

Apart from such forbidden knowledge (and abundant facts about antique porcelain) Max knows much of Will's own history. He shares with him things his father never could or would tell him. Things about his parents' marriage, for example, and about growing up.

'Do you know why your parents named you "William"?' Max asks. 'It wasn't because of your ancestor, the famous convict William Buckley. They named you after William Shakespeare. He lived four centuries ago. A great man and a marvellous storyteller. Took old tales from around the world and made them sing.'

Will mulls this over. Many of Shakespeare's poems and plays are on the Republic's list of restricted works. But Will once thumbed through a small, blue book of smuggled sonnets that his classmates were passing around one lunchtime, behind the bike-shed. His parents had named him after the author of that curious volume? Could that really be true?

Yes, the sharp imagination and intelligent word-play would've appealed to Will's mother. But what could his father have possibly found in the writings of Shakespeare? Maybe the only connection he needed was that the woman he loved found pleasure in those pages. Maybe.

There are other things, too, that Max knows about Will. He knows, for example, that Will thinks about girls most of the time. That's OK, Max tells him, so long as his thoughts are kind and so long as he follows the house rules and does his chores.

And Max shares with Will a secret. He has a guardian angel, who is the soul of someone who died. Such souls, Max says, take every opportunity to peek back into the world. The play of leaves in the wind. The dimness of twilight. The horizon at night. The fog of exhaustion. The deepest, darkest places of the world. Will's inner voice. And the corner of his eye-socket, where he can poke his finger and glimpse the angel's light.

Sometimes the souls do more than just peek, Max says. Sometimes they sneak back into our world. And when they do, he says, they should never be held at bay. They should never be diverted from their journey.

**4**

———

# MILESTONES

T‌ODAY – six weeks after John Page's disappearance – is Will Page's seventeenth birthday. In the dim morning light, he walks along the hallway that connects the bedrooms at the front of Max Bunt's house to the country-style kitchen at the back. Towering shelves and cabinets line both sides of the hallway. Will treads carefully in fear of causing one of the towers to collapse.

As a primary-schooler on holidays, Will had sat in this same hallway and worked his way through the sets of calf-bound encyclopedias that anchored the lowest shelves, while his parents sat at the kitchen table listening to the particulars of Max's latest porcelain find.

'It's truly amazing what you can turn up,' Max had reported. 'Beveridge is always saying there are no more discoveries to be made around Redcliffe, or none worth a damn. That's true, I told him, but only if you stop looking. Actually I'd be grateful if he did stop looking. More for me to find!'

Will pictures the wry smile on his mother's face as she responds.

'Then again, Max, there are many people who would

prefer things from the past to remain marvellously undiscovered. They'd be happy if we *all* stopped looking.'

'I'm not against discovery, Mary, just the foolhardiness of chasing an illusion.'

Everyone in the kitchen is suddenly more serious. The long silence that follows is only interrupted by the whistle of the stovetop kettle.

'Right, then,' Max says awkwardly. And as if by reflex, 'Who's for tea?'

∞

Today, the encyclopaedias are still there, still doing their solid job, despite the efforts of the munching silverfish. Will emerges from his thoughts and the dim hallway to find Uncle Max standing proudly in his denim blue split-leg potter's apron. A metallic red party-hat perches at a jaunty angle atop his head.

*Another funny hat*, Will thinks momentarily.

'Happy Birthday, not-so-young William Page,' Max says, making a sweeping gesture towards the small Formica table.

On most mornings, this table would be home to a row of toast standing tall in a wire rack together with a knob of butter, a jar of marmalade and a small pot of tea. Today, however, it is laden with an extravagance of food.

A pile of pumpkin scones, Will's favourite, sits alongside a plate of crispy bacon, plus home-made baked beans and two fried eggs.

The centrepiece of the feast is a three-tiered sponge-cake with Chantilly cream and fresh strawberries. A healthy dusting of icing sugar over everything – including the tabletop – completes the enticing tableau.

'Sit. Eat. You have a big day ahead of you.'

As Will digs into his breakfast, Max slowly carries a small step-ladder to the corner of the kitchen. He climbs the steps

– they give him an extra foot and a half of height – and he grabs something from the pantry's top shelf. As Max turns around on the ladder, Will sees that it is not another condiment he's carrying but a small package wrapped in butcher's paper.

'Happy Birthday,' Max says, for the second time this morning. After painstakingly descending the ladder, he hands the package to Will, who views it with excitement.

At the end of breakfast, Max clears the plates and Will gently opens his gift. It is a book in a beautiful binding, lettered in gold: THE COMPLETE WORKS OF WILLIAM SHAKESPEARE.

'A smuggler's edition,' Max explains. 'Super-small typeface on micro-vellum. It's Bible paper. I was going to save this book for your eighteenth, but I think you could make better use of it now. So many stories. Histories, comedies, tragedies. Betrayal. Love realised, love thwarted. Duty, bravery, jealousy and the absurd. A whole world of words created in miniature. All these stories passed through the mind of one man, but they were always everyone's, the property of the universe.'

As Will thumbs through the volume, marvelling at the fine print and delicate pages, Max recounts all the different theories that surround Shakespeare and his work. Who was Shakespeare really? Was he an aristocrat, a religious heretic, or perhaps a thief? Did he really write the poems and plays himself, or was he just a frontman for the true author – perhaps for the Earl of Southampton, the Earl of Pembroke or the Earl of Oxford? Or maybe for Bacon, Marlowe, Sherley, Stanley, or even Queen Elizabeth?

'There are people who claim the secret is revealed somewhere in the works themselves – perhaps in a code hidden on a title page, or inside a dedication, a footnote or the index.' Will scrutinises all these in his new book while Max continues.

'Whatever the truth, these texts were recorded at a fascinating time and place. The theatre world was full of cliques and feuds. The English playwrights who fought for fame and renown were as tightknit as they were competitive. Some people say differences are the cause of conflict, but in my book, it's what makes us similar that sets one person against another.'

Will listens as Max recounts local rivalries and obsessions, and in particular his formal and informal competition with Mr Beveridge for the titles of best local gardener, top amateur pastry chef and luckiest treasure-hunter. Will of course has heard this before, but he takes great comfort from Max's storytelling and the certain inescapable wisdom of his perspective on the secret facets of everyday life.

Max and Beveridge had once been very close, and Max reflects on their relationship as he launches into another speech, this time on the true nature of friendship.

5

———

## UNRELIABLE WISDOM

IT IS LATER in the same week. Will is returning library books and running other errands in Redcliffe. Maximillian Bunt is home alone when an unexpected visitor arrives. (Privately Max blames a lidless teapot.) The visitor wears corduroy slacks, a blue checked shirt with a brown cardigan. He looks, overall, very ordinary – like an insurance assessor, Max thinks, or maybe a porcelain collector.

Before the visitor can speak, Max grasps him by the arm and leads him on a flying tour of a domestic library and museum. Shelves of books. Cabinets of curiosities. And case after case of Meissen and Ming and Cookworthy. When the tour is over, Max deposits the visitor on the sofa and offers him tea.

'Earl Grey?' he asks. 'And do you like lemon-butter on your bread? Of course you do.'

As Max makes the tea and the lemon-butter bread, he wonders why his visitor is so quiet, and why he has expressed only a passing interest in the porcelain. Alan Smith, meanwhile, scans the room and thinks of how best to squeeze the octogenarian for information about John Page.

Max returns with the tea and bread, and for half an hour the bachelor and the assassin interrogate each other in their own way. When finally Smith tires of florid, circular, mind-straining stories of ceramics and superstition and small-town politics, he binds and gags his host, then searches his house.

Will Page approaches that same house just as Smith is leaving. Will recognises him immediately as the Actuary he met briefly but terrifyingly in the Chamber of Logic. Gripped by the same fear he'd felt at that meeting, he hides behind a hedge of geraniums and hydrangeas till Smith is out of sight.

When he is sure Smith has gone, he steps towards the front path, then thinks better of it. There is no reason to enter the house now. He has learnt something from his father's theories. He knows that, in one of the rooms, Max is either fully alive or fully dead. God or fate or the universe has chosen one of those realities. Either way, there is nothing Will can do for his uncle now. And he takes hold of a comforting thought. If he doesn't go inside, maybe he can assume the better reality will prevail, or at least remain persistently possible. Surely, he reasons, Schrodinger had an uncle as well as a cat.

Thus reassured, he decides to flee Redcliffe. He will leave Max behind, along with his books, his clothes and the precious photograph of his mother.

Will walks briskly through the centre of town, past Purren's and the emporium, and heads straight for Redcliffe's train station. Greeting the stationmaster, he buys a ticket that will take him as far inland as the train can go. The master hands over the ticket.

'Mustn't forget this, too,' he says, retrieving from the storeroom a backpack Will has never seen before. 'Your uncle asked me to give it to you, if ever you came here.'

Will takes the pack and gives a look of surprise.

'Old bloke's not as dotty as he seems,' the master says wryly, tapping his nose.

On the train, Will explores the contents of the pack. Lemon-butter, fortified bread, pound-cake, sundry other food. Spare clothes. Underwear. A sleeping bag. An army knife. A plastic tarp for collecting desert dew. Hiking boots with thick soles. And a note.

Uncle Max is at least a little dotty, Will thinks. The note wishes him St Jude's luck on his trip, wherever it will take him. Max didn't start the note with the words 'Dear Will' or 'Dear William'. He didn't even use Will's nickname, 'Rabbit'. He started the note, 'Dear Adam'.

When the train reaches the terminus, Will puts on his boots, pockets the knife and continues his inland trek on foot.

He walks all day and well into the night. When at last he stops to rest, he finishes a slice of home-made bread and half an energy bar, then rolls out the sleeping bag and makes a rough bed under a peppercorn tree.

∞

For four whole months the Consistency Engine ponders Professor Macdonald's question. It spins the question round, turns it upside down and breaks it apart. A learning machine, the Engine looks at problems in ways human beings never could, and notices the patterns that human beings miss.

The photographs are certainly a puzzle, and probably evidence of a deeper anomaly. But what to make of them?

The Engine comes to its answer through a chain of logic that is as striking as it is simple. Up till now, the Republic had sent its best, most reliable agents to solve the mysteries of the interior. All those agents have evidently failed. The Republic should, therefore, send an unreliable one.

After digesting this odd-sounding advice, the VC

instructs Mallory, the Bursar, to search the files of the Republican guilds for likely agents. Mallory, though, draws a blank. Not one of the candidates is suitable – or suitably unsuitable. The guildsmen are just too reliable. So Mallory extends his search to the entire database of current and former staff. And he finds the perfect candidate.

'A despicable fellow,' Mallory reports to the VC. 'He can see both sides of every argument.'

**6**

---

## THE PROPOSITION

AT SUNRISE WILL SETS OUT, continuing westward for what feels like many hours till he comes upon a town at the edge of a great grassy plain. A sign on the outskirts gives the town's name as Murnania. Will has never heard of it. Judging by the lacework verandas and the wild-west look, most of the town was built more than a century ago.

Harsh winds sweep along the main street and drive Will to seek refuge in the saloon bar of the largest hotel. Inside, an ancient phonograph plays strange music. The smell of Egyptian tobacco wafts through the bar. The publican greets Will and leads him to a table where he fills a glass from a pitcher of ice water. Will slides into a leather armchair, takes the glass with both hands and empties it.

A weathered plainsman and his daughter are already seated at the table. Each of them gives Will a welcoming glance. The man wears what is evidently the town uniform. Starched white shirt, knitted lambswool tie, narrow buckskin trousers, brown leather boots with pointed toes. The farmer's daughter wears a pale pink dress of thin, close-fitting cotton. Her enamel brooch matches her father's tie-clip and armbands.

The farmer brings Will into a conversation that seems to have been going on forever. Choosing his words deliberately, the plainsman speaks in the musical drawl of the frontier.

He explains what makes a good plot of land. He touches on the subtle features of the terrain that define the world of the plainsmen. He speaks of wars and affiliations and customs, and the histories of factions such as the Horizonites and the Brotherhood, the Webbers and the Sykeses.

Rhythmically the conversation turns from politics to weather, then to saddlery and yields, and to the question of what makes a good and ethical life.

'The measure of a man,' the plainsman says, 'is what he can do with a few thousand acres. How well he can raise a family there.'

The man's daughter nods. She and her father ask Will no questions, but he is fully ready to answer with details of his whole story and the nature of his journey inland, which, moment by moment, feels less and less important. He is fully ready to spill his beans.

Most of the people in the saloon have ordered the same drink, a green spirit. Something apart from the liquor, though, is intoxicating the patrons.

Half in a dream, Will follows the conversation while savouring a remarkable feeling. The feeling of being at home and in the presence of people he has known a lifetime. Waves of sublime relaxation wash over him. He forgets about his parents and the Republic and its assassins.

The maiden looks at Will in a way that deepens the dreamy atmosphere. Will's mind catches and holds the old plainsman's words. The merit in them is obvious. A young man can do no better than to settle down, marry a durable lass, and make a family. It seems to Will that similar conversations are being had at every other table in the saloon – and their harmony serves to reinforce the plainsman's argument.

The maiden is about Will's age, maybe a little younger.

Born and raised on the plains, she knows of nothing else. Her face is suntanned but untroubled. Will notices how she studies his mouth and appears to hang on every unspoken word.

He decides he will stay at the hotel. That way, he can get to know the townsfolk properly, and perhaps scout some promising acreage. Above all, he resolves to begin a courtship. He will buy flowers and a ring with a semi-precious stone for the plainsman's daughter who, minute by minute, grows more beautiful.

The plainsman seems to divine Will's thoughts. After offering to show some of the best properties, the man announces that the Council of the Plainsmen – a group in which he enjoys excellent standing – will host a banquet. The Council will welcome Will properly into the town, and begin his induction into the ways of the plainsfolk.

Feeling a deep contentment, Will begins to plan his life on the plains. Once his homestead is built, he will assemble a great library that chronicles every aspect of the history of the plainsfolk. Their ways and struggles, their leaders and heroes. His children will grow up tanned and happy among peppercorn trees and stooks of wheat.

∞

Outside the hotel, and far outside Will's attention, a dark figure creeps in the shadows. Sidling up to the saloon, the figure appears as a silent silhouette in the doorway, then pauses for a moment to scan the room before making directly for Will's table.

The visitor comes up beside Will and pulls hard at his arm, jolting him to awareness.

'Come *on*,' she urges. 'Snap *out* of it.'

Will Page's junior case officer drags him from his armchair and out of the saloon.

Emerging abruptly from his trance but still feeling half asleep, Will looks back at the hotel and sees two people in hot pursuit. The first is an angry adolescent with matted hair, blistered skin and a jutting, cantilevered overbite. She wears a faded pink smock and is wielding a barstool. Between screams and curses she swears that she'll make short work of Will, and anyone else who jilts her.

An old-timer is the second pursuer. He hops and bounds along on rickety legs, all the while howling and bellowing angrily. He seems to be carrying a real-estate brochure, and a rifle.

Will's stumble becomes a run. He ignores his stitch as the social worker leads him into a maze of backstreets and finally to a lane that ends at a water-tank.

Will and his rescuer hide under the tank till twilight becomes night. Then, in the relative safety of darkness, they set out on foot, westward again through the outskirts of the town and beyond into the plains.

# 7

# NANNY TANNAHILL

EMBARRASSED, Will walks on in silence, his mind pondering the mystery of Murnania. Maybe there's a whole network of such frontier towns and saloons, diverting travellers into mischievous and extravagant traps for purposes that only the Republic fully understands.

Will ponders, too, the equally mysterious presence of his case officer. When his embarrassment fades, he has many questions for her. Why is she here? How did she find him? What will she do next?

The officer introduces herself properly. Her name is Rani Sharma and she is originally from Andhra Pradesh. Now, in her final year of college, she's on a work placement with the Ministry for Social Services in Redcliffe. The Ministry monitors the train station, and that's how she knew he'd left town.

She'd caught the very next train and followed his trail. Her supervisors want her to bring him back. She wants to hear from him about his quest. Then, she says, she'll make up her own mind about what to do.

Rani gives Will a summary version of her life story. Growing up as an only child in India. Moving to Australia as a teenager. When she arrived, the first people she met were social workers. So, naturally, she thought of becoming one.

In her first year at college, she pledged to look after the people who would come into her care. She took that pledge seriously then, and she does so right now insofar as it applies to Will Page. She also takes seriously the Republic, and the dangers it poses for truants and heretics.

Despite the case officer's beauty, and even though she rescued him, Will is wary. Rani's loyalties seem split between him and her masters. Her rebellious streak is obvious – so strong it reminds Will of his mother. But Rani is respectful, too, towards Republican authority. Gambling that he can trust her at least to some extent, Will explains why he is travelling inland.

The reasons are many. His mother disappeared there, and perhaps his father, too. For better or worse, his ancestors made their names there. And none other than the eminent Oliver Macdonald himself saw evidence of a desert enigma: the mysterious photo of the girl with the ice-cream.

Will doesn't let on about how he saw Macdonald and the photo. That's just too risky. But otherwise he recites all the reasons for his inland trek.

When he first set out from Redcliffe, those reasons made perfect sense to him. Now, though, as he recounts them to Rani, they make no sense at all.

Not one of the explanations he gives is convincing on its own. Putting his motives into words makes them sound ridiculous. If he were more self-aware, he would know that his true motive is much deeper and more mysterious. A silent, inexpressible call from the centre of the continent. A call that draws him ever on, beyond all reason and common sense.

Unable to convey this call to Rani, Will feels a new kind of embarrassment. Rani, though, smiles encouragingly and says she will join him in his quest. The best way to fulfil her pledge, she says, is to travel with her client, or patient, or whatever he is.

'Wherever you're headed, and whatever it is you're going through, I'll help you get through it.'

Though he doesn't say so, Will is infinitely grateful that Rani, and not her tall, fair-haired supervisor, was the one to come after him. But he suspects her motives are more complex than she lets on. Perhaps she feels pity for a hopeless case. Perhaps she delights in the adventure of it all, an escape from her ordinary, routine work.

Part of Will, too, can't entirely banish the idea that she is spying on him, or fulfilling some other kind of secret purpose.

∞

As the pair set out further inland, Will keeps his doubts to himself.

Initially he and Rani walk mostly in silence. Then Will begins to share with her some of the stories his parents told him when he was young. Stories about the interior and its rich and mysterious history.

Like the one that Will's mother used to tell, about her great, great grandfather, William Buckley, who, almost seven feet tall, was said to have shaved with a scythe. As a young man, Buckley fought in France against Napoleon. On his return to England he was wrongly convicted of handling a bolt of stolen cloth. Sentenced to transportation as a reward for his service, he escaped from a colonial prison. In the ungoverned region west of Port Phillip, an Aboriginal family welcomed him as an ancestor – returned, blanched, from the dead.

Will also shares the story of Louis de Rougemont, another ancestor, who battled giant octopuses, enormous sharks and a living sea of rats, and who, when his ship went down in a cyclone, was towed ashore by the captain's dog Bruno, the hound's tail clenched firmly in the Frenchman's teeth.

Will's father had told old stories, too, but those ones were darker and less fanciful. Will could never forget the one about the grazier, John Horrocks.

Lured by enchanting tales such as Buckley's and de Rougemont's, Horrocks travelled far inland looking for lakes and rivers and woods and pastures – a vividly imagined garden of delights. But all he found was desert and disaster. A camel accident caused his rifle to discharge. The stray bullet destroyed the middle fingers of his right hand before entering his cheek and knocking out a row of teeth. His injuries turned septic and he died in agony and bitter regret.

*Harsh*, Will had thought, when he first heard that story. *Death by camel.*

Then there was Ludwig Leichhardt who, two years after Horrocks, led a well-equipped party into the interior. The entire party – seven men, seven horses, fifty bullocks, 270 goats – disappeared.

Will tells these stories, along with the one about a farmer named Coulthard, who set out in 1858 to find the same delights that Horrocks and Leichhardt had imagined. Coulthard's mummified body was later found, along with a message scratched into his empty water bottle.

'My eye Dassels. My tong burn. I can see no More. God Help.' Those words were seared into Will's memory.

Rani in her turn shares stories – fictional and factual – that she learned from her parents and during her childhood in India. Modern stories of nation-making and nation-breaking. Harrowing accounts of famine and poverty. Ancient stories, too, of Shiva and Vishnu and the thousand-headed snake Shesha.

Rani's words are amazing, Will thinks. So unbelievable

and yet so compelling and powerful. To him at this moment, they seem more real than the terrain.

∞

As the travellers walk in this talkative fashion, the country opens out before them into dry grasslands of cooch and spinifex and serrated tussock. The hard and sharp grass-blades tear at Will and Rani's shins, forcing them to adopt a serpentine route that follows irregular tracks around the spiny clumps. When, more than a century earlier, de Rougemont came upon this very same spinifex, he called it porcupine grass.

Every few kilometres there is a cluster of scraggly trees. Will counts them out loud and bounces over them in his mind. After three days of sharing stories and bouncing over trees, the pair come upon a remote farmhouse. Having learnt from the experience of Murnania, they approach carefully, using bushes and old farm equipment as cover.

There are two people on the veranda: an old woman and a tall, thin youth – possibly eighteen, definitely playing a concertina squeeze-box. As he heaves at the concertina, the woman cusses and swears at him. Then he breaks into a tune that Rani and Will find haunting, sombre, unfamiliar. When mercifully that melody ends, an equally mournful one follows, then abruptly comes to a stop when the woman yells again.

'This ain't no foon-eral! Liven it up, boy. Be damned with 'em dirges!'

The lanky youth bobs his head, flexes his fingers.

'As ya say, Nan. As ya say.'

A lively medley of jigs follows. Grapevine Reel. Walk in the Parlour. Old Joe.

The woman's face cracks into a wide grin, exposing amateur dental work. She foot-taps along, until the tapping turns into pounding. And then she is on her feet, twirling and prancing with lifted skirts and kicked up heels. As she trips and dips and pirouettes, her tangled grey locks work themselves loose from their bun, fanning out over her shoulders. Her eyes sparkle and a bloom covers her cheeks. The music has possessed her.

Will and Rani watch in silence, fascinated by the creepy spectacle, neither of them willing to break the woman's trance. After two more songs, Will whispers to Rani that they should reveal themselves. Rani urges caution. The pair argue back and forth for some time until the old woman suddenly stops her singing and dancing.

'Why not just come over ere,' she says formally, 'and we can discuss this together?' The woman is fading in many ways, but her eyesight and hearing remain impeccably keen.

Tentatively the travellers step forward from their ineffective hiding place.

'I'm Nanny Tannahill,' the woman says. 'This ere's Remus. Only desert past my 'ouse. Best turn round. Lotta folk get lost round here, specially young folk. Or maybe you'd care ta stay. Always work ta be done. Extra 'ands never go astray. Couldn't pay much, but I keep a trim house. Tidy is as tidy does.'

Noticing the rubbish and old ploughs and fridges that fill the yard, Rani and Will exchange a sceptical glance. Nanny keeps speaking – to distract the travellers from Remus's twin brother Romulus, who sneaks up behind them.

Though lanky like his brother, Romulus possesses remarkable strength. The crooks of his elbows are like vices, and it is with these that he grabs Will and Rani by their necks.

The captives put up a fight but Romulus is too strong. Remus joins the fight as well. All the while, Nanny shouts instructions and encouragement.

'Don't shilly-shally! Get their damn legs!'

Will, fighting on two fronts, notices Rani on the ground, senseless. Then he, too, receives a stunning, disabling blow.

Pain.

Stars.

Nothingness.

8

———

**THE BASEMENT**

INTO A HOUSE DECORATED with cow skulls and taxidermed hares, the Tannahill boys drag their victims, then hump the prone bodies downstairs before chaining them by their wrists to a cinderblock wall in the foul-smelling basement.

When Will and Rani come to, they realise they're not the only captives. Chained to the opposite wall is a monstrous boy who looks like a genetic experiment gone terribly wrong. If a mad scientist ever spliced the genes of a pot belly pig, a Murray cod and a human being, that unnatural hybrid might come close to what Will and Rani now see.

They are unsure if the boy is a Tannahill or a captured traveller like themselves. They detect no family resemblance between the Tannahills and the boy. But there is no resemblance, either, between him and any living person.

The boy has a wide, pale face with a deep, sloping forehead, a flat nose, and thick, pinkish lips. His stubby head accounts for a quarter of his mass. The waxy pallor of his flesh gives the impression of damp and viscosity. His muddy blank eyes convey an inhuman lack of emotion and intelligence.

Judging by his height, he is no more than twelve years old. The length of his chain marks out a radius of food-scraps and other waste. The boy seems to have been chained up for a long time. He and his surroundings are covered with the same thick patina of muck.

Through that veneer, though, Will and Rani can still see the bruises that cover his arms and legs. And they can also see, just out of reach, the kangaroo-thigh bludgeon that Romulus and Remus grasp whenever they're in the basement.

Like a mad creature, the growling and spitting boy pulls at his chains and kicks at the floor. Will senses in him, though, a primitive cunning, even a capacity to manipulate his captors. At dusk, Remus delivers a pile of scraps. The boy – Romulus and Remus call him Grig – seems to feign weakness the whole time his captor is present. He seems, too, to be exceptionally alert to every movement Remus makes.

When the youth returns upstairs, Grig returns to the task of pulling at his chains. Will and Rani take stock of their surroundings and their plight. The Tannahills have confiscated their packs along with Will's watch and army knife. Things seem hopeless. And what terrors might follow? What do the Tannahills have in store for their prisoners?

The grotesque boy, the noxious basement, the terrifying outlook. For Rani, these bring to mind every horror movie she has ever seen. But the spectacle that confronts her is dreadfully real. Desperately fearful for herself and her charge, she scans her surroundings with razor intensity. Then suddenly she makes a face, as though she's had a brainwave.

She shuffles over till she's right up against Will.

'I've been meaning to do this,' she says.

Reaching down, she grabs one of Will's thick heels with both hands and twists it off, revealing a cavity and, wrapped in tissue paper, a small knife. The other heel also contains a hidden cavity and, within a little metal sheath, a little miracle: a miniature pistol and a cache of miniature bullets.

'Thought those heels looked suspiciously thick. I've seen boots like these before, in my training. Kids use them to smuggle contraband into boarding schools and reformatories.'

Will is amazed.

'Thank you Uncle Max,' he says under his breath.

He and Rani re-hide the knife and the gun. Once night has fully fallen, they take turns, one keeping watch, the other using the knife to harry the masonry around the bolts that hold the chains to the wall. Grig watches for a while, then curls up on a bed of filth in the farthest corner of his end of the basement.

Now in good spirits, Rani whispers jokes while poking at the masonry.

'What do you call hillbillies who live hundreds of miles from the nearest hill?'

After an hour, the bolts come loose. Still carrying their chains – Will and Rani plan to get far enough away that they can use the pistol to blast open their manacles – they creep up the stairs, then tiptoe along the hall.

Will's heart is beating so hard he can barely breathe. His inner voice tells him to *hurry, hurry, hurry*.

Just inside the front door there is a wobbly table and a tin tray full of plunder. Silently Rani retrieves her gold bracelet. Will can't find his watch but he grabs his army knife.

On the porch, the escapees find their ransacked packs. Carefully they pick them up, trying not to jangle their chains. Then they dash, as best they can, into the night.

After running about two miles with their burdens, Will and Rani stop half way along a rocky gouge. Will bends over, his hands on his knees, his lungs burning, his muscles screaming as loudly as his conscience.

Stripping off the pack, he turns and bounds back along

the gouge, his feet slipping and sliding in the gravel, his chains flailing and clanking.

'Will!' Rani shouts.

He keeps going, not looking back.

'Will!'

Her voice trails after him and is lost in the wind.

At Nanny Tannahill's house the lights are still on. Will loops his chains round his shoulders, then approaches the northern side of the bungalow. Passing under the kitchen windows, he hears Nanny cackling and singing to herself.

'Hey do! Merry do!'

She is busily sharpening knives, no doubt in preparation for what she thinks will be her morning's work.

Grasping his small pistol, Will creeps up the steps to the porch, then opens the old-fashioned fly-screen door. The rusty springs and hinges screech as he slips inside. Gingerly he inches along the hallway. When a floorboard creaks his heart skips and adrenalin surges through his arteries.

He opens the basement door and tiptoes down the stairs. Grig is still chained to the wall, still curled on his filthy bed. Will reaches out to wake him. Only then does he realise the boy is fully awake already, and fully capable of tearing Will apart. Grig seems, though, to understand why Will has returned. He seems, too, to have decided to play along.

Using Will's army knife, the boys take turns working at the chain-bolt. Every now and then, Will whispers nervous and unnecessary remarks, like 'Don't make a sound' and 'Be careful'. Soon the bolt is loosened and Will again escapes from the Tannahill basement, this time with Grig in tow.

When the escapees reach the farm boundary, Grig makes a crude sign of acknowledgement and peace. Then he gestures for Will to go. He himself will return to the farm-house and settle up with the Tannahills.

Will rendezvouses with Rani. The little pistol makes short

work of the manacles. Blissfully free of their chains, the pair walk in darkness till they come upon an old frontier fort. There they rest, before travelling further inland.

9

―――――

# TRAVELLING COMPANIONS

Nanny Tannahill told many lies, but one thing she said was true. The country beyond her house is indeed desert.

Over sand and gravel, Will and Rani walk and walk. In the punishing heat of midday, they imagine – or hallucinate – armies of shadowy figures in the distance. At night, Will sees a different army, one of lights that dance just above the horizon. For over a century, the lights have been called 'min-mins'. Among the original inhabitants of this land, they have much older names. For Will, the dancing lights bring to mind the rival beliefs of Uncle Max and the Republic. He is sure min-mins aren't part of Mandelbrot's Complete Periodic Table.

As best they can, Will and Rani continue in this fashion. Will loses track of how many weeks the pair have walked through scorching days and freezing nights. Not that the cold is the only reason why, at night-time, he sleeps close to Rani. As close as possible, without it being too obvious. Sometimes their sleeping bags brush against each other. Whenever that happens, Will feels a little charge of electricity pass between the two wrapped bodies.

∞

Mr Smith, the shadowing murderer, might've used the same words. *As close as possible, without it being too obvious.* He has no immediate plans to kill Will Page. Rani, too, is not yet in his sights. Smith will follow the pair till they lead him to the boy's father. Only then will the killing start.

Every Actuary is trained from infancy to become an expert in stealth and murder. Smith is a leader among the Actuaries, a master of all their arts. Here, though, in the flat expanses of desert, he can't stay completely hidden. No-one can.

As a child, Smith had entered the Hanging Rock Monastery. In the subterranean silence of the monastery's halls, he excelled in every test set forth by his masters. Soon no-one was his equal, except perhaps his brother. In a paradoxical way, the Smith brothers stood out. They distinguished themselves by being utterly indistinguishable – from each other, more so than if they'd been identical twins, and even from their peers.

Thinking back to those days, Smith has an unsettling thought. Was the brother he had at the start of his training the same one he had at the end? He doesn't mean this metaphorically – he was trained to despise metaphors – but very literally. It is fully possible that his brother was any one of his fellow initiates.

As Smith watches Will and Rani make camp, he has an even more troubling thought. *Perhaps my brother is me and I'm the one who became someone else.*

∞

Will and Rani sense Smith's presence, and on occasion he is more than just a presence. At night, they sometimes see his fire on the horizon, brighter and steadier than the playful min-mins. When Will and Rani lose their orientation, they sometimes circle and come across one of his campsites. And then they sharpen their navigation and quicken their steps.

The relentless presence of their sinister pursuer causes an intolerable feeling of dread. The companions are soon confident, though, that Smith is not an imminent threat. After that realisation, they do their best to ignore him. Ultimately, the terrain rather than Smith brings Will to the limit of hope and endurance.

When he reaches that point, Rani is very much in his thoughts. A vivid memory of when he first saw her on Uncle Max's doorstep, her white dress slightly see-through in the bright sunlight. And equally vibrant mental images of what he hoped he might one day share with her. Images of dancing and swimming and laughing that had sustained him on the relentless trek. Now, though, the dominant, debilitating thought is that all those dizzy imaginings will come to nothing.

'I'm sorry I brought you here,' he says grimly. His voice sounds remote, as if he's half conscious. 'Should've turned round weeks ago. Should never have left Redcliffe. We've got to go back.'

Rani, just as tired, studies Will's face and seems to be carefully processing his words, the first he has spoken about turning back.

'I think,' she says, 'we can go a little farther.'

**10**

---

# THE THEORY OF EVERYTHING

A_S THE PAIR WALK_, Rani considers the travellers' predicament. How can they conquer this terrible landscape and their mounting despair? There is a way, she decides. They have to keep swapping stories.

She kicks off with the tale of how she and her parents first came to Australia seeking a verdant land – precisely the opposite of what she sees before her at this very moment.

In actual fact she'd wanted most of all to go to England, the land of Jane Austen and Mary Shelley and Virginia Woolf. She loves those authors' books, and their heroines and heroes who puncture pomposity and people's everyday nonsense. The characters who imagine a different way of living, and who have the courage to bring it about. All her favourite books are stories of transformation and escape.

When migration to England proved impossible, Rani and her parents settled for their second best hope. Australia. Rani shares with Will the delight she felt when, soon after arrival, she won a place at a good college.

She shares, too, her encounters with ignorance and prejudice. In her work at the Ministry she is eager to help and succeed. She has tried to fit in, to adopt the conventions and rituals of her office. She makes sincere and smart suggestions about doing things differently, to better the lives of the people of Redcliffe and nearby Newstead and Campbell-town. More often than not, though, her suggestions are ignored. On bad days, Rani thinks her colleagues and supervisors barely even notice her presence.

Most disappointing of all is the dead hand of the Republic, the institution she reluctantly serves. She has seen the harrowing insides of its prisons and reformatories. Against her own values and judgement, she has helped enforce the rules of Consistency.

∞

When it's Will's turn to speak, he begins by sharing the story of his father, the country boy made good. This story, too, is one of change and escape. And it is a story Will shares with pride.

Unlike most of his fellow Redcliffians, John Page was always destined to leave town. At the age of seven, he was already preparing for bigger things.

A natural born scientist, he studied with fascination the properties of gasses and fluids and solids. If he could get his hands on any kind of device – an old record player, a sewing machine, a mantle clock – he took it apart. His singular mission in life was to find out how things worked. Particles and waves. Planets and galaxies. Time and space. He would interrogate reality and uncover the truest truth.

At the age of nine, he estimated the circumference of Planet Earth. Correctly.

'But who told you how to do that?' his amazed teacher asked.

'No one.'

'But how'd you do it?'

'I watched the moon, from the bottom paddock. The sun, from the water tower. Did a few sums.'

A few very clever sums, it turned out.

'But *why* did you do it?'

'I just had to know.'

These words would be repeated many times in the Page household. They became the heart of a great family story. But when the same story got around Redcliffe, more than a few people were sceptical.

'Must've cheated,' busy Mr Beveridge said. 'I wonder what he was *really* doing, spending all that time in the bottom paddock.'

Despite the scepticism, though, the story was true – and John would display the same determination to win a place at Sandstone University, home of the best physics department in the hemisphere.

For country people like John Page, the annual scholarship exam was the only way in. Would determination and brain-power be enough to take him from a small town to the centre of science and culture? In the exam room he was all confidence, even though the stakes were so high.

The final question on the exam was about the Theory of Everything.

All the students dreaded that question. The Theory is notoriously complex and devilishly difficult. It brings together the whole universe. All the physical forces, all states of matter – including dark matter and dark energy – at every physical scale. Everything from the enormous totality of the cosmos right down to the smallest particle and the tiniest, quivering string.

The foremost achievement of modern science, the Theory showed once and for all that planet Earth revolved inconsequentially around one of a hundred million stars in a spiral arm of an unremarkable galaxy. Just a tiny mote of dust in the vast accident of space-time.

When the Theory was first verified, all the textbooks had to be rewritten. To express the new facts, the new books borrowed words from Mark Twain.

'How insignificant we are, with our pigmy little world! An atom glinting with uncounted myriads of other atom worlds in a broad shaft of light.'

The famous cosmologist, Professor Guy Cherry, expressed the same thought more bluntly.

'The human race is just a chemical smear on a moderate-sized planet, orbiting a very average star in the outer suburb of one among a hundred billion galaxies.'

The Theory shook things up at the microscopic scale, too. Particles only wondered at before – hadrons, muons, gluons – were now no longer hypothetical. They were part of science.

The Theory was so powerful, so all-encompassing, that it explained all history. Every war since the Stone Age. Every invention and innovation. And every step in humanity's journey around the globe, right up to Captain Cook's discovery of Australia and the arduous mapping of the continent. Everything fitted together beautifully.

So beautifully, in fact, that the leaders of the Republic adopted the Theory as their manifesto, enshrining it into law. Deviations from the Theory were banned by official decree.

The ban extended to all physical heresies, like geocentrism and flatearthism. All historical ones, too – such as divergent accounts of wars and civilisations – and zoological ones, like minyips and bunyips.

Republican censorship also silenced the oral histories of Australia's first people. Ideas of sacred places, 'songlines' and 'dreaming tracks' had no meaning for the leaders of the Republic, for whom untilled and undeveloped land had no value, spiritual or otherwise.

Everyday heresies – the old superstitions about hats,

shoes, umbrellas and knocking on wood – were also doomed. The Theory swept away such barbarisms and old wives' tales just as thoroughly as it replaced the old science. Even history itself was said to have come to an end, a thing of the past.

For his answer to the final question, John Page wrote out fully and elegantly the mathematical proof of the Theory. In other words, he nailed it.

Now armed with his physics scholarship, seventeen-year-old John moved from Redcliffe to Port Phillip.

In his first tutorial at Sandstone, he pronounced 'wondering' as 'wandering' and rhymed 'compromise' with 'promise'. He had, after all, gathered much of his vocabulary from books. His fellow students called him a hayseed.

But he studied hard and graduated with distinction, before returning triumphantly and temporarily to Redcliffe, where he took up a senior lectureship at the local college. It was there that he met a beautiful graduate student.

Mary Buckley.

Tall. Single-minded. Self-assured.

If John was obsessed with science, then Mary's obsession was Australian history. *Unorthodox* Australian history.

Her family went back a long way in the antipodes. She claimed descent from some of the most colourful nineteenth-century pioneers. Thanks in equal parts to her heritage and her personality, Mary was ever ready to embrace the ideas that people in authority rejected. The most surprising myths and doubtful legends – these were what most intrigued her.

From librarians and other old-timers, Mary heard the same strange tales that had so beguiled early travellers such as Horrocks and Leichardt. And she believed them.

Word got around that Mary was a yippy, one of the hopeless cases who swallowed doubtful accounts from the early exploration of *Terra Australis*. Stories of inland seas and marvellous gold reefs. Man-eating plants, giant reptiles, flying marsupials and other impossible creatures.

The yippies were utterly disreputable, their beliefs in clear opposition to the Theory. But Mary became their most convinced and committed member.

In its mapped and colonised form, Australia was a product of the Enlightenment, the scientific revolution. If, Mary thought, there were errors in the continent's history, then that would be of worldwide scientific importance. This was the focus of *her* search for truth.

Mary first saw John Page in the college cafeteria. Within a few short moments she'd measured him up and worked him out. In an eerie way she could read his thoughts on his face.

'The best window to the soul,' she would later say, quoting a famous philosopher. And she noticed how, with a show of false confidence, John stood with an uncomfortable straightness that would rather be a slouch.

He for his part was enchanted by her stately, austere beauty, but also her alertness and independence of mind. Society disapproved of her ancestry and her beliefs, she didn't care what society thought, and society didn't know how to respond when she ignored utterly its disapproval.

The courtship was intense, the marriage swift, and Will was born soon after.

11

―――――

## RABBITS DON'T SWIM

WILL'S own life story began with simple pleasures. Growing up in and around Redcliffe, just as his father had done. Catching cicadas and skinks. Fishing for yabbies in the dam. Swimming in the creek. Gulping down clean, lemon-scented air under impossibly wide skies.

Just before his seventh birthday, Will was chasing wild rabbits on the town's outskirts when he cornered one against a kidney-shaped dam. Creeping up to the panting creature, he was certain he'd catch it.

The rabbit, naturally, had other plans. It leapt into the water and swam to the other side, shook itself off, then ran full pelt into the bracken. Will ran home, too, to share his surprise with his parents.

When he'd finished telling his story, Mary smiled and turned to John.

'He's probably telling the truth,' she said.

But John was plainly unimpressed.

'Nonsense,' he said in his most serious lecturer voice. 'Rabbits don't swim.'

A blatant falsehood had come from his own son's mouth.

What a disappointment for the scientist who put such store in the quest for truth.

Seeing the disappointment in his father's eyes, Will sprang to his own defence. The rabbit really had taken to the water, he said, and had dog-paddled or rabbit-paddled at a cracking pace.

But John wouldn't budge. Will went to his room, fighting back tears, stung by the unfairness of it all, glad his mother had taken his side.

The next day, he repeated the story at Redcliffe Primary, a school of no more than a hundred pupils. That's how Will got his nickname. Tim Weston gave the story as much credence as everyone else at the school. But he was the only student not to call Rabbit Page a liar.

Tim had a nickname, too. For reasons never explained but universally accepted, everyone called him Loopy. Eleven years old, he'd been held back twice. Now, therefore, he was four years older than Rabbit but only two grades ahead.

Loopy was the product of a mixed marriage. His father, a retired lawyer, and his mother, a ballerina from a travelling dance troupe, had married for love.

The marriage appalled Redcliffe's townsfolk, as did Mrs Weston's habit of opening her front door in her birthday suit. The government, too, was unhappy. Unequal marriages were an affront to the principle of Consistency. People, the Republic said, should stick to their own kind.

For Loopy, the marriage was a disaster. Children from mixed unions weren't allowed to prosper. They were barred from the best jobs and denied the best opportunities. In work and society, Loopy would never get far.

And yet despite all this, Rabbit and Loopy were often seen together. After school they swam in the Loddon River and yabbied in Muckleford Creek. Loopy taught Rabbit the proper way to catch yabbies, not with mutton and twine but with brute force and lightning reflexes.

The boys were almost inseparable – until John won a professorship at his old university and moved again from Redcliffe to Port Phillip, this time with his wife and son in tow. Except on school holidays, Will was no longer Rabbit.

∞

In the physics department at Sandstone, John Page flourished. He filled his lab with a stunning array of equipment. Lenses, clocks, mirrors, scales, magnets, compasses, astrolabes, jovilabes, micrometers, thermometers, barometers, condensers, computers. In the afternoons and evenings, Will would often watch his father working away at his experiments. John was utterly in his element.

Mary joined the university, too. The history department gave her a research job – on condition that she abandoned her unconventional beliefs and interests. From now on, she promised, she would toe the line.

That promise, of course, was always going to be broken. First in the library and then in the field, she explored the heretical mysteries of El Dorado, Lasseter's Reef, the Mahogany Ship, the Dutch Beards, the Tahitian Jews.

And the Bellarine Keys. These iron artefacts were discovered on a beach to the south-west of Port Phillip. Covered by metres of sandy, limey sediment, they must've been there a long time.

A very long time.

In fact, someone must've dropped them on the beach more than two centuries before the official history books said this coast was first discovered by people with the technology to make metal implements.

Were the keys evidence of earlier exploration of Australia, even earlier occupation, perhaps by the Portuguese? The mystery soon took a sinister turn. The keys disappeared and the lime-digger who found them was murdered.

Naturally, Mary suspected a cover up – a suspicion that strengthened her foremost conviction: the published history of Australia was a fiction.

As the Chancellery lost patience with Mary's obstinate disobedience, they applied more and more pressure. Her in-tray of official warnings and reprimands bulged. But she stuck to her studies and convictions.

At Sandstone, young academics were allowed to challenge their superiors to debate scholarly matters in a public forum. The debates were modelled on the thrilling tournaments of renaissance Italy, in which mathematicians and magicians battled each other.

Apart from fostering scholarly excellence and competition, the debates made the top professors seem more accessible, more human. For the challengers, the stakes were incredibly high. Winners saw their careers leap forward. Losers risked their careers evaporating.

Held in midwinter, the duels were timed to celebrate the solstice. As soon as she was able to, Mary put herself forward confidently – some said audaciously. She would waste no time with small fry. She nominated the most senior academic as her opponent.

Mary was so sure of herself and her research, so committed to her life's course, that her confidence did not wilt, not even the slightest little bit, when she learned the Vice Chancellor, Professor Oliver MacDonald, had accepted her challenge.

When the moment came for her to mount the stage, Mary pulled out her secret weapon: Louis de Rougemont's personal memoir of his exploits and discoveries.

She read out extracts, such as his description of a bloated, man-eating tree, and his account of the Mkdos tribe, 'little known but cruel'. She painted vivid word-pictures of men and women riding on the backs of turtles, shooting native bows and arrows, and going into battle – on stilts.

Then it was the VC's turn to speak. Carefully, cogently, he demolished Mary's arguments and de Rougemont's memoir. He presented incontrovertible proof that the book was entirely made up, an elaborate hoax.

'Where we now know there is barren desert,' the VC said, 'Monsieur de Rougemont claimed to have found beautiful fountains, rustic perambulators, great gold nuggets, and – least likely of all – vineyards! His journal was published at the end of the nineteenth century. In the years that followed, he embarked on a book tour, and was universally denounced as the world's greatest liar. This,' the VC said with a flourish. 'This is the authority to which Dr Page resorts.'

The very next day, the Chancellery tore up Mary's contract and sent her on her way. She was ready, though, with a new project: an epic trek to find gold and glory in the centre of the continent.

She would retrace the steps of Lasseter and Buckley and de Rougemont, and prove once and for all the truth of their claims. She would put the disaster of Midwinter behind her.

As soon as she made her plans known, every kind of crazy entrepreneur and adventurer and swashbuckler stepped forward to join the expedition. Some of the applicants had energy and money. She invited the best of those to join her.

Keith Drayton was one. A technologist and futurist (Will wasn't entirely sure what that meant), Drayton was driven by the prospect of finding industrial quantities of gold. Michael Smith also joined the expedition. He, too, sought treasure, but was also motivated by science. Or so he said.

Amadeus Zouche joined as well. An eyebrowless million-aire who craved excitement, he paid for most of the party's equipment and all the porters, who were led by a small, bookish, tight-lipped man called Noakes.

Calmly, patiently, John Page had counselled against the venture. All he could see in it, he said, was danger and disappointment. He marshalled every kind of argument. And he shared his fears about Australia's dead heart.

'The European history of the Pacific Ocean is all about people finding things they weren't looking for. Hawaii. Tahiti. Aotearoa. The European history of central Australia is the opposite: a story of people failing to discover what they sought. The continent's interior is one big dashed hope. A shattered dream.'

Mary, though, pressed on.

# 12

# REMAKING THE WORLD

WHEN THE REST of the world lost contact with Mary and her hodgepodge crew, John Page put Will into boarding school and went looking for her. Afterward – a long time afterward – John told Will that no trace of the party could be found.

Will was almost too young to understand what it meant to be lost in the central desert. Almost.

John returned to his role in the physics department. Will returned to the day school, before starting at Ashburnham High. Every holiday, though, Will went back to Redcliffe. Back to his nickname and to his friendship with Tim Loopy Weston.

The boys egged each other on to ever greater escapades. Loopy was always stronger, but Rabbit did his best to match his friend in races up Big Hill, and in sprees through the granite crevices of Chewton Mine.

John Page didn't approve of the friendship. Probably no respectable father would. But he saw what it meant to Will, and he knew that having an older friend around – perhaps not as smart, but possibly as wise – might be good for the boy who thirsted for friendship. Especially now that Will had no mother around to guide him in life, and to tell him he looked handsome at his school formal.

The heat, though, soon came out of Will and Loopy's friendship. For reasons neither of them fully comprehended, something happened between them that changed their relationship forever.

The boys still played together on holidays, and no-one else noticed the cooling off. But Will felt less and less comfortable with the friendship, and more and more nervous in Loopy's company.

And then Loopy moved to Port Phillip, and the boys had their awkward reunion. Though Loopy joined Ashburnham as the new cleaner, he preferred the American term, janitor. Either way, he still had to mop up a vast daily mess.

John's career, too, saw an abrupt change of direction. He decided to move from the mainstream of physics to its speculative edge. With this shift, his enthusiasm for science only increased.

He made the shift at the height of his standing and intellectual power. It would bring him, he said, closer to how the world really worked. It would also bring him closer to trouble.

The accountants and engineers who ran the university had a grudging tolerance for physics. They reasoned that Sandstone's physicists might one day do useful work, just as Wilhelm Mandelbrot had done when he first verified the Theory of Everything. And the physicists' mind-bending math deserved respect, to be sure.

But this grudging tolerance was especially thin for the speculative branch of physics, a branch that John now grasped firmly.

He began speaking in a strange language about 'local and shared realities', 'collective time', and 'zones of inconsistency'. He conducted screwball experiments and produced scientific papers with titles that could've passed for counter-culture bumper-stickers. 'The irrelevance of scale.' 'Hamlet and quantum indeterminacy.' 'Paradox and everyday life'. 'Planning for chaos.'

If his work continued in this direction, he'd be drummed off campus, just as Mary had been. It was only a matter of time.

∞

Will shares most of this tale with Rani, but he leaves out his cooling off with Loopy. That part of the story is too awkward, and painful. When he is finished telling his stories, Rani smiles sympathetically. She can see what they mean to him – especially the precious ones about his mother.

'You're a good listener,' Will says.

'It's my job.'

After a contemplative silence, Rani speaks again.

'I have another story to share, if you want to hear it.'

'I do.'

Absentmindedly Rani spins her bracelet round her wrist.

'When I started college, my parents were so proud. They'd sacrificed so much and I'd worked so hard. After my first semester, I won a scholarship. It came with the opportunity to stay on campus and take additional units in the School of Psychology.'

Rani's mother had wept all the way to her daughter's dorm room. It was pride, she said, more than sadness. Rani's father had mostly remained stoic, but even he spent more than a moment that day pinching his nose and wiping away moisture from his eyes. The family had been through so much together and had never been apart. That first night at college was the first time Rani and her parents had slept under different roofs. For Rani this was terrifying. Isolating. Exhilarating.

The college curriculum was a smorgasbord. Rani took

extra classes in the fundamentals of human behaviour and human learning. Her stellar grades caught the attention of her senior lecturer, Dr Sandra Cooper, who invited Rani to assist in lab work and experimentation in her second year. Usually, opportunities like that were only offered to graduate students. But Rani was exceptional, and Dr Cooper proved to be a wonderful mentor.

Cooper stressed the human side of psychology and social work. She implored all her students to support, nurture and understand the people in their care. She was interested in the real world and the whole person. For her, psychological theories were just empty vessels, to be filled with the real-world experience of practitioners.

The students got used to hearing the Cooperism, 'A life lived by the rules of science alone will leave you as useful as the textbooks you hold in your hands. Full of information but bloody useless for anything except holding open a door. And instead of holding the door open, a real healer walks through.'

Rani's parents often visited her during the school year, especially on weekends. The family would meet for a home-made tiffin-stacked lunch on the grass of the quadrangle. Rani would share the stories of the week and her dreams for the future. Perhaps, she dared to hope, there might one day be a place for her in the faculty – once she'd filled her cup with experience.

When Rani reaches this point in her story, her blood drains from her face and she is suddenly grave and exposed.

'Before my third year of college, my parents and I went for a driving holiday. On the highway, north of Port Philip, there was an accident. A bad one. A truck crossed into our lane and forced us off the road. The steel barrier did nothing to slow us down. We hit a tree head-on at full speed. I was in the back seat. My parents were in the front and they took the force of the impact. They didn't make it. That's one reason why I took up the placement in Redcliffe. To start anew. To put the horror of the accident in the past.

'There was one small mercy. My mother regained consciousness for a time. While we were waiting for the ambulance I held her in my arms. I nursed her, gently pressing my lips to the top of her head, just as she'd done for me whenever I was ill.'

Rani had known in her heart that these would be her last moments with her mother. The pair would never again talk of Rani's week and her plans for the future. Leaning back into Rani's shoulder, her mother had felt so small. This woman who'd been such a powerful force in the direction of her daughter's life was suddenly so fragile.

'As she closed her eyes, she told me to be true to myself and our dream. The dream of making a new life. And, even in a small way, the dream of remaking the world in a better shape.'

# 13

## A HARD BARGAIN

THE NEXT DAY, Rani and Will continue their westward journey. Normally they would rest during the hottest hours. But today there is no shelter so they push on.

Beyond the ever-shimmering horizon, faint sounds of tack and harness reach the travellers' ears. Will and Rani exchange glances.

'Do you hear that?' Will says. 'What is it?'

Rani drops to her haunches, turns her left ear to the sound and makes a thoughtful face.

'I don't know'.

She can't get a fix on where the sound is coming from. She and Will think momentarily of hiding or fleeing but there is nowhere to hide and nowhere to run. And in this great open expanse, the cause of the sound is just as likely to pass them by as to move into visual range.

So the two just stay where they are, in a bind.

Of course, uneventful journeys are meant for uneventful people with uneventful lives, and neither Will nor Rani is destined for one of those.

Soon, something large and odd emerges from the blurry horizon. At first it is shapeless, like a dark figure glimpsed through wet glass. Then it has more shape: it is a hydra whose many large heads bob rhythmically from side to side on long stalks. And finally it appears as it is: something no less strange but perhaps less fantastical than a mythical beast worthy of Jason and his Argonauts.

A well-dressed, powerful-looking woman fills the seat of what Will can only describe as a wagon-cart-caravan-train. In front of her, at the head of the procession, five camels lurch. And immediately behind her there is a large enclosed wagon whose roof is tiled with tarpy lumps of what appear to be merchandise. Further back in the train, an open cart holds two bullocks and a penny farthing bicycle.

As this striking parade nears Will and Rani, the woman gives a smile and doffs her bowler hat. A sign on her main wagon reads, MAGNIFICENT MARGARET'S MYSTERIOUS AND MISFIT SOUVENIRS.

'Started out in the final days of the Golden Age of Alliteration,' the woman explains, perhaps noticing Will's careful review of her carnivalesque signage. 'Kind of ran out of steam at the end, but you know how it goes.'

Will is quite sure he doesn't know how is goes, but he thinks better of saying so.

Magnificent Margaret – for that is who she says she is – jumps down from the wagon and, moving in a fluid manner that belies her strong frame, pulls the lever that protrudes just below the harness that connects the yoke to the wagon and thus the camels to the whole peculiar tableau.

The bowels of the wagon emit a grinding metallic murmur that suggests some sort of mechanism has been triggered. Will and Rani step instinctively back. They've learned something from Murnania and the Tannahills and they're determined not to be taken by surprise.

Eventually the whirring stops.

Nothing happens.

'Blasted contraption,' Margaret complains as she thumps the side of her wagon.

There's a clatter. Perhaps a ping. Maybe even a whizz.

A second forceful intervention of meaty fist on wagon frame does the trick. The square side drops open. Sprightly flagpoles spring to attention at each of the four corners. Flags of red, green, blue and orange catch a breeze that, until now, had not existed.

Inside the wagon the door mechanism has formed a set of uneven steps. Beyond this perilous entrance there are shelves and racks that strain and bulge with all manner of bric-a-brac. Pots, pans, bell jars, glass buoys. Amidst the chaos, Will spots something that is both impossible and, by now, inevitable.

A tarnished silver frame. And inside, a photograph. In the slightly soft-focus light of a studio portrait, a man and a woman stand shoulder to shoulder, smiling. A small boy, perhaps six years old, sits immediately and contentedly in front of them.

As Will reaches with determination for the photo, Rani's eyes follow the stretch of his arm. She sees the face of the sitting boy. His smile is familiar. She has glimpsed it only a handful of times, but she has definitely seen it before.

'It's you,' she says.

Will has no memory of the photograph but he nods in agreement.

'And that's your mother and father,' Rani says quietly as she shifts to stand hard by his left shoulder. 'I recognise them from your file.'

Will nods again. His heart is racing and he feels the world rush away in a sudden moment of vertigo. Rani places a steadying arm around his shoulders.

'Ah, a beautiful frame that,' Margaret says as she climbs into her showroom.

Scrambling over piles of homewares and curiosities like a

waterfowl crossing lily pads, she snatches the photo from Will's grasp. He curses his reflexes.

'Sterling silver,' Margaret announces. 'Can tell by the hallmarks.'

Nimbly she exits the wagon and squints at the back of the frame in the sunlight.

'The tree, the fish, the bell, the lion rampant. They tell you everything. It's from Glasgow in Scotland. Was assayed there, too. It's proper official silver. Can't quite make out the imprint letter. That would give you the year. But look at this head. Belongs to Her Royal Majesty Queen Victoria. The duty on this piece was paid in the nineteenth century. Now that's gotta be worth something.'

From inside the wagon, Will watches Margaret's performance while still pondering the photo. She continues her flamboyant scrutiny.

'There's the maker's mark. J. & P. D. Now that's the most interesting thing about this particular piece. Must be why I got it in the first place. There's a great story attached to it.'

∞

Magnificent Margaret, it turns out, knows a lot about old silverware. And she knows a lot about the Douglas brothers, James and Peter, who were both skilled silversmiths.

During the mid-nineteenth century, Glasgow was on its way to becoming a centre of industry. It was also a nascent metropolis, plagued by overcrowding and pollution and squalor. Like many other European cities of its day, Glasgow was riding the wave of automation and mass production driven by steam-powered machines and the ingenuity of the industrial revolution.

James Douglas was the elder brother. An idealist, he saw modern invention and manufacturing as blights on true craftsmanship. Mass production was a false prophet that spelled mass doom for the people who vacated the Scottish countryside and filled Glasgow's streets and boarding houses and brothels.

The younger brother, Peter, was James's equal in every way save that where the elder Douglas saw the end of humanity, the younger saw limitless possibilities. In the march of progress, the world was shrinking. Goods that came into existence at one corner of the globe could be at the opposite corner in ten months. Eight if you were canny about shipping. The new reality of a smaller world gave Peter Douglas big ideas.

The brothers had four members of staff: a senior craftsman, two apprentices, and Elizabeth Selby who, from August of 1869, came twice a week to clean the Douglas's small but endlessly cluttered offices.

It didn't take long for James to take a shine to young Elizabeth. But he was a fair-minded fellow, who recognised it would be ungentlemanly and unprofessional for him to press his feelings upon Elizabeth while she was in his employ. Instead, he would admire her from afar, as it were, and help her by making sundry acts of anonymous kindness.

Elizabeth for her part was certainly thankful for those acts. A Christmas ham, quietly ordered by James for her parents and six siblings; food enough for a week, actually two, given how her mother made stew. When Elizabeth's baby sister fell ill with a fever, James silently paid for a physician to visit.

Like many of Glasgow's poor, Elizabeth lived in a crowded close of flimsy cottages. In the winter of 1869, her home was under threat. The Glasgow City Improvement Act was about to bring 'improvement' to the metropolis. Elizabeth's neighbourhood was slated for demolition to make way for important civic works: modern wonders of iron, steel and stone.

This time, another Douglas brother came to the rescue.

When Peter heard of Elizabeth's plight, he cut straight to the heart of the matter. Mr Wathergill was the proprietor of the city's most successful brickworks. He was also chair of the Chamber of Commerce and he had an advantageous relationship with a Mr McCrae, a senior surveyor in the office of town planning. Peter struck a deal with Wathergill, who would intervene with McCrae on the silversmith's behalf.

The intervention couldn't halt the demolition of Elizabeth's home – the Improvement Act was unstoppable. But Peter and Wathergill were able to stall the wreckers until the following summer. In return for this help, Mr Wathergill received a small stake in the brothers' silver business.

The new partner was experienced in the mass production of clay bricks, and Peter saw this as an opportunity to modernise the Douglas's operations – perhaps even to apply the principles of mass production to the craft of silversmithing.

Upon hearing of his younger brother's actions, James was appalled. He was also furious. The sudden appearance of a new business partner was maddening, to be sure, as were the implications for the future of the business that he co-owned. But perhaps worse still was the style and scale of Peter's generosity towards Elizabeth, which went far beyond anything James had dared to venture.

Certainly Elizabeth couldn't fail to know of Peter's help. Certainly, too, she was grateful for it. Over time, that gratitude turned into admiration and, possibly, love. She adopted the habit of asking after Peter's health before James's. And she would linger for extended periods by his desk, whether he was present or not.

One evening, as he was leaving the office, James noticed that Elizabeth had tied a ribbon from her hair around the handle of the small gaslight on Peter's desk.

In a turn of rage, jealousy and spite, James stoked the fires in the workshop and set about melting every finished piece of silver and every raw ingot that the brothers had in stock. Pouring out the molten metal all over their offices, he set every scrap of paper and every piece of timber alight.

As the flames crept higher, James strode from the building, leaving everything to the hungry flames.

No one knows for sure what became of the Douglas brothers, but a few details are known about Elizabeth. Without the income afforded by her cleaning work, she had to take whatever employment she could find. For a time she found it at Mr Wathergill's brickworks, which always had need of hands to tend the kilns, and which was expanding, rumour had it, thanks to a large injection of recovered silver.

The next summer, shortly after the demolition of her family's home, Elizabeth disappeared. Pragmatists and realists concluded that she succumbed to the circumstances and perils of her era. But romantics and storytellers prefer a different tale, one that ends with Peter reuniting with Elizabeth, and the two of them running away to Australia, where they lived out their days surrounded by grandchildren in an Eden of their own creation.

∞

'So, what's the offer,' Margaret says, placing the picture-frame face-down beside her. 'Surely such a storied piece warrants a hefty price?'

'I'm really just after the photo,' Will says, reaching out for the prize once more.

Margaret lays her hand across the frame, clicks her tongue to the side of her mouth, examines the back once more.

'Job lot, I'm afraid. The catches have oxidised. Couldn't open it even if I wanted to.'

Will has no memory of the photograph, or the day that must have been wrapped around it, but he is desperate to hold and contemplate the image. At a loss, he offers to trade his pistol, his army knife and his heel blade. Not surprisingly, this little ensemble fails to pique Margaret's interest.

'I sure ain't no trader,' she says philosophically, 'if there's nothing to trade.'

Will feels the earth beneath him sway, until Margaret opens up a sliver of hope.

'What about you, young Miss?'

'I'm afraid I have even less than Will. Neither of us really packed for this trip. And we certainly didn't expect to barter.'

'What about that?' Margaret says, pointing to Rani's side.

Rani's left hand reaches for the gold bangle that decorates her right wrist. Instinctively she turns it around several times before studying its simple geometric patterns.

'For something as delicate as that,' Margaret says, 'I might be interested in parting with my pretty frame.'

Rani hesitates before answering. Hearing echoes of breaking glass and screeching tyres, she is suddenly serious.

'Throw in a camel and a month's worth of supplies and you have a deal.'

When Will looks at Margaret's camels he recalls the accident-prone beast that doomed the grazier Horrocks. He can't help but make a disbelieving face.

'Ah, at last we're haggling!' Margaret shouts as she slaps her thigh. 'One week's supply and my penny farthing. I've been saving that blasted contraption for paved roads, but I ain't never seen one of those for the better part of ten years.'

Rani shakes her head.

'Three weeks and a camel. We have no need for a bicycle, especially one that's barely built for one.'

Margaret's eyes flit between the golden bracelet and the leathery figure of her chief camel. Cantankerous, stubborn Oscar. Unsentimentally she contemplates the shape of his mid-section, notes the prominence of his spine and ribs, does some calculus.

'Two weeks and my best camel. I'll even throw in some tack. Because I like you. Ain't got no saddle, but you should be able to make do.'

Rani takes the bangle from her wrist and holds it out to Margaret. Will notices that his case officer is looking anywhere but at the bangle.

'You have a deal.'

∞

As Margaret helps load the supplies on Oscar, Will asks her about the bullocks. Surely hauling livestock in these conditions is a liability.

'Midas and Mithos are there for the rainy season. Camels don't work in the mud but bullocks do.'

Alarmed, Rani asks when the last wet season was. She pictures the monsoons of her childhood in India.

'Oh, there ain't been one yet,' Margaret says conspiratorially, shaking her head and whistling through her teeth. 'But I'll be ready when it comes.'

Will wraps the picture-frame in old clothes, then tucks it snugly into his backpack. After a brief farewell, he and Rani and Oscar head west. Margaret heads south. When she is only just in earshot, Will calls out:

'MEMENTOS!'

Margaret stops her caravan, gives a confused look and shakes her head. In light of her triumphant, one-sided trade, and now this shouted contribution from Will, she is questioning the sanity of these two odd travellers who are heading into the heart of nothingness.

Making no reply, she starts up again and her procession is soon fading into the obscuring heat. Then Will and Rani hear an ecstatic cry. Perhaps it can be best described as a holler.

'Well I'll be! MISFIT MEMENTOS indeed!'

# PART II

---

## INLANDIA

# EXTRACTS FROM WILLIAM BUCKLEY'S DIARY

# AUSTRALIA FELIX, 1835

They have no notion of a Supreme Being, although they have an afterlife, as in my case; and they do not offer up any kind of prayer, even to the sun or moon, as is customary with most other uncivilized people. They have a notion that the world is supported by props, which are in the charge of a man who lives at the farthest end of the earth. They were alarmed on one occasion when I was with them, by news passed from tribe to tribe, that unless they could send him a supply of tomahawks for cutting some more props, and some more rope to tie them, the earth would go on the run, and all lands would be smothered. Fearful of this, they began to think and enquire, and calculate where the highest mountains were, and how to get to them, so as to have some chance of escape from the threatened danger.

# AUSTRALIA FELIX, 1836

The bunyip defies description. Viewed from one side, it resembles a buffalo. From another, a large octopus. Though mostly aquatic and somewhat fish-like, it is far removed from dolphins and whales. Covered with fine, dusky-grey feathers, it takes confidently to land. In its bulk it exceeds the hippopotamus, yet it is remarkably agile and can conceal itself with startling speed. The local families employ bunyips to clear seagrass and waterlily from the margins of estuaries, and to push trails through dense scrub. I have no doubt the bunyip could be put to even more extensive use. Above all, I am certain it could pull a plough.

## 14

**THROWN IN**

Weakened and despondent, Will and Rani foresee no happy ending to their inland trek. They've lost all hope that they'll find anyone or learn anything. They could blame God or the universe for their predicament. They could curse their luck. But instead they just walk.

Though the terrain is now more difficult, the journey has also become more beautiful. Every night, the travellers see many of the Milky Way's hundred billion stars. That vista makes Will and Rani feel as irrelevant and inconsequential as Professor Cherry's thin, chemical smear.

In the daytime, Will and Rani walk under a painted sky. They traverse a desert bereft of oases but abounding with wild camels – descendants of John Horrocks' lethal beast. Not long after Will and Rani had parted company with Magnificent Margaret, they decided Oscar, like the batch of rancid 'supplies', was a bad trade. They released him, with all good wishes, to join the wild herd.

Apart from camels, Will and Rani encounter emus and bilbies, along with sleek bluetongues and leathery shingle-backs. Despite these residents, though, the landscape is surprisingly empty. And startlingly silent. There is a feeling that something dreadful has happened here. A great sweeping away of people who had a deep and rich past. People who once owned this land and maintained a bosom connection to it. Just by walking through this country, Will feels implicated in a terrible crime.

From time to time, he and Rani notice hints that the terrain might be about to change. Suggestions of an end to the relentless flatness. Perhaps a rise or, better still, a valley and a creek. But the valleys are all phantoms, the creeks illusions. The country is so flat that – surely a paradox – the travellers think they can see the curvature of the earth.

Mile after mile, under a searing sun, Will and Rani trudge over obstinate dunes and interminable stony plains. Angry, scorching winds slice across the sand and the rocks. The landscape itself seems to oppose the two intruders. Traversing the resistant and unchanging terrain is like walking on a hellish treadmill.

If there is any real change in the landscape, and that is doubtful, it is the subtle sense that the land is becoming ever drier. Over tens of kilometres the red sand does in fact become dustier, the sun harsher. The centre of Australia is a hotplate and Will and Rani are being cooked.

And then, imperceptibly at first, the texture of the ground begins to change. Ever so gradually, the blank desert sands give way to grass and tiny shrubs. And then to footprints and other signs of people.

Soon the ground in all directions is covered with little yellow flowers. The travellers can't believe their ears when they hear the sound of running water. Nor can they believe their eyes when they come upon a clear, wide, fast-flowing, stony-bottomed river.

Beyond the river they see a gently sloping hillside with clusters of cottages connected by handsome aqueducts and separated by leafy trees. Beautiful villages bathed in amber light. And in the distance, impossibly large, a golden pyramid – an incomprehensible, otherworldly spectacle for people who, only moments ago, were trapped in a lethal wasteland. Will and Rani are awestruck.

The hills angle upwards to a distant escarpment that forms an immense natural amphitheatre. The river snakes southward to a large lake, or perhaps an inland sea – it is hard to tell as the far shore is beyond the horizon. Wide-sailed fishing boats like Arabian dhows ply the shallows. A tall lighthouse stands on the shore, and rich orchards and vineyards spread out between the lake and the villages. The scene reminds Will of Rivendell and Neverland and other marvellous places he has only ever read about in storybooks.

The houses nearest the shore are shingled with abalone shell and mother-of-pearl, which catches the light in a dazzling way. The same light sparks diamonds on the surface of the river, from which Will and Rani drink hungrily. The water, the mild air, the mind-blowing spectacle, the feelings of accomplishment and relief: together, these seem to do something magical to Will's stamina, and even to his physique.

His mind immediately clears and he feels energised, more muscular, and taller. In actual fact he *is* taller, and not just because of his thick-soled boots, not just because he has instantly lost the inherited tendency of Page men to slouch.

Rani, too, is transformed. The whole time she has lived in Australia, others' low expectations of her and her fellow migrants have weighed her down. Now, those expectations have fallen away. Her eyes brighten and she becomes even lovelier than before, the princess she was always meant to be.

Noticing the changes in themselves and each other, Will and Rani beam with delight.

∞

After resting for more than an hour, Will and Rani hear a clamour of voices on the far bank. They look across and see, in the middle of a crowd, a tall man with broad shoulders and a long beard. The man wears a leather tunic and sandals. He is about forty years old and doesn't have a pleasing face – somehow, despite his beard, his face is all mouth. And it's an angry-looking mouth.

Above his head, the man holds a small, red-haired, freckly girl, probably no more than nine years old. The girl is screaming.

Twenty people look on as the man throws her forcefully into the broadest and deepest section of the river. She lands about five metres out and quickly the current takes her. Will and Rani can see her struggling, and sinking.

'She's going to drown!' Will shouts.

He dashes forward and leaps into the river.

Rani follows close behind.

Will swims as fast as he can but the quick current is carrying the girl away. Just as he catches up to her she disappears below the surface. A deep breath and Will follows her down.

Deep down.

Irrationally, frighteningly deep.

Three metres below him, Will sights the girl, her arms spread wide above her head as if to embrace the body of water that now rushes over her.

Will kicks hard and propels himself downward. Soon the girl is almost within reach and he can see her face, framed with electric hair that radiates as though reaching out to her rescuer. But once more the current takes her and she is pulled out of reach.

Incredibly, Will has seen the girl before, in the photograph at Sandstone. Will has found what legions of agents and fleets of drones could not. The Cottingley fairy. The ice-cream girl.

With a final desperate kick he reaches and grabs her and they tumble and twist in the water. Will is suddenly gripped by panic. He has lost his bearings and can no longer tell which way is up.

Suddenly he remembers a trick that Loopy taught him. You can let out a little burst of air and follow the bubbles. They always travel upwards.

But Will has been breathing out all the way down. His lungs are empty. And then Rani is beside him. She points in a direction and helps Will carry the ice-cream girl to the surface. As soon as they break through, Will holds the girl as high as he can in the choppy water. Her eyes flutter open and Will is relieved at this sign of life. Folding an arm around her midriff, he drags her towards the nearer bank. Rani swims beside them, aiding whenever Will struggles.

In equal parts surprised and enraged, the tall man tracks the trio along the riverbank and waits for them to reach the river's edge. When they arrive he grabs Will and the girl by the scruffs of their necks and drags them from the water, dropping them roughly on the bank. Rani climbs out and runs to embrace the girl.

'What's your name, little one?'

'Jenny,' she says through tears. 'And I'm not that little. I'm more grown up than I look.'

The bearded man regards Will menacingly. Judging by his expression, he would happily throw the intruder back into the water – or somewhere much worse.

'What shall we do with you?' the man asks. 'We don't get many youngsters from the Outland. Let's see what the Queen makes of you.'

He gives a beckoning signal and two men break off from the crowd. They wear the same style of tunic as the man they call Lord Krull. They seem to be his lieutenants. On the opposite bank, fishermen gather Will's backpack while on this side Krull and his men steer Will and Rani and Jenny along the snaking, white-granite path that leads to the pyramid.

# 15

# AN AUDIENCE WITH THE QUEEN

JENNY QUICKLY RECOVERS from her rough baptism. As Will and Rani soon learn, she is used to being the brunt of random acts of cruelty.

All the way to the pyramid she gives an upbeat narration, like a proud and welcoming tour-guide.

'Our country is called Inlandia, or Mkdos – the Middle Kingdom. We call ourselves the Mkdoans, or the Mkdorii. We live in villages on the shores of the lake. This village is Quincampoix. Our families are large. I myself have five half-brothers and two step-sisters. We play cricket and lacrosse. My father is an expert at throwing knives. And,' she says with regret, 'children. Our citizens have come from all around the world.'

Some of those citizens emerge from their homes and yards to see the captured travellers. An oldish man in a reddish kaftan. A fisherman in short shorts. A woman dressed like an Amazon and holding a pearwood bow.

Rounding a corner, the guided tour comes upon a bewildering sight. Pulling a cart in the opposite direction along the path is a desperately strange example of Inlandian megafauna.

The creature is a kind of hairy, feathery, aquatic ox. It is like nothing Will and Rani have ever seen before. Not at Port Phillip's zoo. Not even in a book. For at least the third time this afternoon, they are dumbfounded.

Jenny notices their surprise.

'That's a bunyip,' she says. 'We don't eat them. They're sacred, you see. Very useful, too. We also have minyips, which are much smaller. They're sacred, too. And great pets.'

Along the way, the group moves in and out of the shadows of tall aqueducts that are supported by towering archways of grey flecked granite that is coloured with lines of quartz and, on the southern sides, patches of orange and green lichen. Where the afternoon shadows are deepest, Will detects a faint phosphorescence in the lichen.

As the party nears the great pyramid, Will can see it is made from massive blocks of gold, each one perfectly hewn, each one evidently ancient but beautifully preserved. The captors and their captives enter the monument at ground level through a columned porch and tall doors carved from thick pine. Guards carrying halberds flank the entrance.

The doors open to a grand chamber decorated with royal crests and painted portraits. Will notices on one side a sumptuous display-case of relics, all of them relating in some way to William Buckley or Louis de Rougemont. Buckley's shaving scythe. De Rougemont's copy of John Bell's *Principles of Surgery*, in four volumes. A walnut jewel-case. And a small, bronze dog – a likeness of Bruno, the valiant hound who saved de Rougemont's bacon.

The group passes into a second chamber lined with dark velvet drapery that seems to suck up all sound, creating a cold stillness, an atmosphere of waiting. Violently the lieutenants push Rani forward and throw Will down on the golden floor in front of a dais, upon which sits the Queen of the Middle Kingdom of Inlandia.

The height of stately, aloof beauty, the yellow-haired,

hawk-faced Queen wears a suit of pearl armour and, on her long fingers, a dozen golden rings.

Krull speaks first, adopting a tone that is the closest he can come to respectful. In front of the Queen, he is always on his best behaviour.

'Two Outlander spies, your Highness. Caught interfering with Spartan business.'

'You threw me in the river!' Jenny interrupts. 'And they saved me!'

'My step-daughter is feeble, your Highness. The runt of the litter, so to speak. A dunk in the river is a Spartan test of strength. Helps toughen up our juveniles. She needs it more than most. An especially slow runner and poor fighter. Altogether too *Athenian* in her interests. With all due respect, your Highness.'

While Krull is speaking, Will's eyes fix on the Queen's. Then the warrior falls silent. He, like everyone else in the chamber, has noticed the significant exchange of wonder and acknowledgment between the monarch and the boy.

Will's studio portrait of his parents was one of his most precious possessions. Now, in the pyramid, he can see that Mary Page has aged barely a day since she sat for that picture.

Mary, too, recognises her son right away. She sees in his face her own features and those of her husband. The line of his jaw. The fan of his ears.

Will picks himself up and runs towards his mother. Royal guards with clanking pole-axes intercept him.

'Let him through,' Mary commands. She rises from her throne, descends three golden steps and embraces the son she hasn't seen for more than five years.

The embrace lasts more than a minute. Eventually the pair part, smiling.

'This is bonkers,' Jenny says. 'What *is* going on?'

'She's my mother,' Will explains.

'Thanks a lot! Might've told me you were famous.'

The Queen gives instructions to her Secretary.

'Inform the court and the parliament that my son has arrived. His Royal Highness, Prince William.'

Then she turns to Will.

'You shall have the freedom of the palace, and the library, and the gardens.'

Will's smile broadens as the Queen leans forward and says, in a hushed tone meant only for him, 'And you can see your father, too.'

# 16

## AN INCONSISTENT PAUSE

THERE IS much talk and frantic planning. The palace administrators buzz about, making arrangements to accommodate in short order this unexpected addition to the royal household. Within the fortnight the prince will need a royal reception and a private audience with the Queen. Within a day he will need somewhere to live, and people to wait on him. And in due course, as part of his formal induction into Inlandian society, he'll have to meet the Teacher.

Lord Krull offers Jenny as a ward and attendant for the new prince.

'You snatched her from the river,' Krull says darkly. 'Now you can be responsible for her.'

After an hour of administrative shuffling, Rani is led away to meet the Queen's ladies in waiting. Will is taken to the golden pyramid's dungeon. Two of the Queen's guards lead him down four long flights of stairs that end at a damp hall. The hall smells of rubbish and is lined with dozens of bushroach-infested cells, all of them with occupants other than the roaches.

The guards open a barred door to one of the cells and invite Will to enter. As soon as he does he is grabbed and embraced by his father – the father who fully expected never to see Will again. Another long hug.

'I've so much to tell you,' John says when the hug is over. 'And so many questions to ask.'

Will notices that John, too, had been transformed by Inlandia. Fitter, stronger, younger, he is back to his former professorial self. In fact, his eyes seem brighter than before, his mind even sharper. Will glances around the cell. No sign of peach-tins anywhere.

John explains how he came to be in the Middle Kingdom.

'It's a dangerous journey,' he says. 'I know that more than most as I've made the trip twice. The first time was a failure. The second brought me here. Most people never get even a fraction of the way. The Republic uses all sorts of tricks to confuse and confound travellers. Furphies, traps, diversions. The intention seems to be to hold people at the frontier, or to send them back to the coast.'

Murnania and the Tannahills come to mind for Will, but he mentions neither of these near-misses to his father. John is eager to tell his story, and Will is eager to hear it.

'I suspected I might find *something* in the middle of the continent,' he says, gesturing at his grimy surroundings and the jarringly opulent golden walls, 'but nothing . . . nothing like this.'

At breakneck speed he speaks of how his research challenged the unity of reality. And of how, although Consistency drives what he calls 'shared reality', inconsistency is also abundant.

'That,' John says smugly, perhaps slightly bitterly, 'is how I found your mother.'

Will purses his eyebrows, makes a quizzical face.

'Ever since she disappeared, your mother has been the focus and goal of my research. I knew she'd become utterly convinced of something that was demonstrably false. So I followed a train of thought. What must reality be like for her to be right? The double-slit experiment showed contradictory facts about light could co-exist. Simultaneously, light is both particles and waves. Such things are possible in the strange world of quantum physics, where the rules of Consistency can sometimes be suspended. But that world exists only at the tiniest of scales and energies – not very helpful for understanding the nature of everyday reality.'

Enthusiastically, John speaks of strings and waves and dark matter. Even allowing for the unique way in which his father talks, this all sounds to Will like gobbledegook. It reminds him of the worst parts of John's presentation to the baffled citizens of Redcliffe.

Perhaps, Will thinks with alarm, he has misread his father's state of mind. Perhaps the former professor is still in his mental funk. But, little by little, as John continues to speak at a thousand miles an hour, Will starts to make sense of what his father is saying. Most clearly of all, the pieces start to fall into place when John describes a particular experiment.

'It all starts with the wristwatch I built. It has a quantum switch of my own design. At any given moment, the position of the watch's second hand is affected by the decay of a tiny piece of radioactive metal inside the switch. That way, a quantum event can be projected on the watch-face.'

Will thinks back to one of the times he visited his father's lab at Sandstone. He remembers seeing John tinker with a peculiar looking box attached to the back of the timepiece. He also remembers John's washing-line, time-measuring contraption in Redcliffe. Instinctively he looks at his own wrist, only to remember the Tannahills stole his watch.

'Strictly speaking,' John says, 'before it was observed, the quantum second hand didn't *have* a position. Every time I checked the face, I was observing the results of a quantum event. Each one of those times, I noticed a tiny but detectable pause. The pause was an important giveaway, a hint of deeper processes. With every observation, reality composed itself and the watch selected a time to display. In physics, we call this trembling, pregnant moment the collapse of the quantum wave function, an event brought about whenever a human observer makes a measurement of a quantum state. After that brief interlude of reality sorting itself out, the watch would tick normally and consistently at one-second intervals. But here's the marvellous thing. I discovered that *all* clocks behave the same way. All clocks have that same tell-tale pause when first observed – even if they don't have a special quantum switch attached.'

# 17

# A HICCUP IN REALITY

'For decades,' John explains, 'science has distinguished between the way matter behaves at the tiny, quantum scale, and how it behaves at the macro level of people and planets. This distinction is crucial to Mandelbrot's Theory of Everything. My discoveries, though, debunked the distinction. On clock faces, the strange rules of quantum physics were already in force at a scale that was relevant to everyday life.'

As John speaks, Will notices how excited he is. The delight his father felt at the time of his clock discovery is back with him now, animating and inspiring him in his dank prison cell.

'The discovery opened the door to many more mysteries. The time that is shown on a clock face is not just a personal thing. When multiple observers come together with multiple clocks, it is possible to synchronise them. It is possible, in other words, to have a common, agreed time. But how can that be if every clock shows a time caused by an individual, idiosyncratic, quantum event – an individual collapse of the wave function?'

This is where, according to John Page, society collides with fundamental physics.

'In my watch experiment, there was a single observer. But in most real-world situations, multiple observers interact. They do so through language and culture and power – the things that collectively we call society. Perhaps, I thought, society was what achieved Consistency across the different clocks.

'I arranged a follow-up experiment. A dozen subjects would participate in what I said was a psychological study. They would be assessed according to a personality test that sorted them into psychological types, such as Judgmental Analyser, Messianic Introvert and Diligent Narcissist. I told the subjects they had to synchronise their watches constantly, right down to the second, so we could accurately document the study.

'The superficial experiment told me much about the subjects' personalities. The underlying experiment told me much about how those personalities influenced the watches – not just their own ones, but in some cases every watch in the room. I repeated the experiment with new subjects. In each new round, the results were the same. The shared time was decided by the watches that belonged to the most charismatic and dominating subjects. The Messiahs and Narcissists mostly. Perhaps, I thought, this could happen on a larger scale, too. The most forceful observers in a group; the most powerful orators or theorists or ideologues. Maybe *they* determined the collective time. And, by logical extension, the collective reality.'

Will pictures John's experiment in his mind. Each of the watch-checking subjects dominating or being dominated by the others, not understanding that they are centre stage in a study that could undermine the Theory and change the world.

'Which brings us to Inlandia,' John says. 'If reality is made through societies and other groups, then people *outside* those groups ought to be able to persist with inconsistent beliefs, in inconsistent realities. This is the real breakthrough I made. In the mathematical equation that defines how the universe works, reality itself is the variable.'

Will fossicks in his mind for examples of flexible reality.

'Like a dream,' he eventually says.

'Yes but not a random or disconnected dream. The world is a dream that follows rules. Each of us is an observer who weaves a local reality, whether dreaming or awake. Each of us is a reality generator, marshalling fundamental particles or strings into coherence. Then, the mechanism of Consistency knits those personal realities together. The knitting happens socially, through conversation and debate. Every time people meet, there is a contest of realities. After every such contest, the dominant reality prevails.'

Will continues his effort to understand what his father is saying. John describes how he has identified many zones of potential inconsistency. Zones in which multiple realities can be tolerated and physical contradictions can persist. Madness is one such zone, childhood another.

'No one takes children seriously,' he says. 'At least, not enough for them to shape reality on a large scale. Not enough for their own reality to become dominant. They do play a part, however. Highly improbable events are part of the everyday experience of childhood. Next time a child claims to have seen a dragon or a rhinoceros in the back garden, don't discount it out of hand. The child may well be telling the truth. The creature could be there as part of a local reality.'

Will imagines Dürer's rhinoceros, clad in splendid armour, gambolling in a suburban vegetable patch. He has experienced first-hand the kind of disbelief his father is describing. The episode with the swimming rabbit at Redcliffe is still raw.

'Animals, too, aren't taken seriously,' John says, 'though they're better observers than we are. They're immune to human culture, so they probably see the strange uncertainty that surrounds every one of us. Little eddies and multiplications in reality.'

Animals, children, dreams and miracles. Quantum physics and hypnotic trances. All these are on John's list of zones of inconsistency. Certain dusts and potions, too, can cause hiccups in reality.

'My experiments reached a critical point,' he says. 'I began to suspect that a massive inconsistency might explain your mother's disappearance. I hatched a plan. With the right method, I thought, I might be able to perceive contradictory realities, even move between them. That would be a perfect way to prove or disprove my theory – and to find your mother. Arriving at the right method, though, was difficult. I couldn't use quantum physics. That would be too dangerous. I couldn't rely on childhood, of course, and I refused to take any sort of potion. The only way was through a kind of madness. I had to do something dramatic. I had to become Hamlet.'

18
—————

## OF HAWKS AND HANDSAWS

WILL HAD READ *Hamlet* among the plays in the Complete Works. He remembers the famous soliloquy, and the protagonist's increasingly unhinged behaviour, which had such a destructive impact on the people around him. And he remembers, too, the forbidden book of sonnets, and Uncle Max's praise for their author.

'If reality is about power,' John continues, 'then I had to break out of the Republican power structure. Only then could I perceive and participate in a different reality. I had to unlearn what I thought I knew, and society had to form a different view of John Page. I had to become . . . unreliable.'

'Hence the public lecture,' Will says, with more than a tinge of relief.

'I was fumbling in the dark. At first, I thought changing reality would be straightforward, that all I needed to do was to change the perceptions of the people closest to me.' John reaches out and cradles Will's face between his hands. 'And that meant you, my son. Mistakenly, it turns out, I set about discrediting myself in your eyes alone. You see, I thought that would be enough. And I really didn't give a damn about what anyone else thought. All that mattered was who *you* thought I was.'

Will feels the back of his neck flush as he remembers how he felt when his father disappeared.

'But that definitely wasn't enough. I misjudged the level of external influence required to shift my reality. I needed more people to doubt me. And I needed to doubt myself. Only then could I change my own perception bias. Only then could I jumpstart a new reality. I'm sorry I couldn't explain that to you at the time, that I couldn't share with you what I was doing, and why. But bringing you into the secret might've undermined the whole plan. It could've blocked me from entering Inlandia, just as I'd been blocked on my first trip to the interior. I didn't know how everything worked. Even now, I'm still getting my head around it.'

After his lecture at Redcliffe, John had set out for the exact place where he'd lost Mary's tracks.

'I thought it would be too dangerous to bring you. And I knew you'd be safe with Max.'

This time – his reputation trashed, his self-confidence shaky – John was able to cross over into Inlandia.

Father and son sit quietly as Will digests what his father has told him. The permanence of truth and reality: that was the foundation of physics and philosophy. Ever since ancient times, scientists and philosophers had made an assumption, implicitly or explicitly, that, once a physical fact or law had been proven, it would always be true.

A freshly opened skull would always reveal a brain. A telescope pointed at the full moon would always show craters and seas. The features of Planet Earth would forever line up with the Republic's authoritative maps. Or would they? John's work, and the reality of Inlandia, showed the possibility of something entirely different.

'Hamlet said the proof of his sanity was that he could tell a hawk from a handsaw,' John says. 'But what if an observed object could be both things at the same time? And if that were true of objects, then could the same be true of people? Of places? To misquote those famous words, could they both be and not be?

'In the laboratory and then on foot, I've discovered a radical property of the universe. The flexible nature of reality is why the Republican drones haven't found Inlandia. It's a real place, but – from the point of view of a reliable Outlander observer – it doesn't exist.'

Will thinks of his father in Redcliffe. At the lowest point of John's decline, Will's own perception did indeed shift, but the shift wasn't absolute. Through his own memories of who his father was, Will had created a kind of back-up, a failsafe version of the man he loved and respected. And that man is now with Will, in person and in full flight.

John's theories of reality are the defining achievement of his career. They are as electrifying as they are unnerving. If true, they explain a lot. The placebo effect in medicine, for example. Also telepathy. And ghosts. Many of the phenomena behind spiritualism and religion. And the sensation that, for no apparent reason, household light switches sometimes change position overnight.

As an immediate proof of his theories, John points to the occupants of the dungeon.

'You,' he says, 'are a great example. All children can enter Inlandia, so long as they make it through the punishing desert. So, too, the pitiful wretches who wander the desert, addling their brains with dangerous potions and aethers, keeping dehydration at bay just long enough to stumble upon Inlandia. Lunatics, too, sometimes make it here. And,' he adds ruefully, 'discredited theoretical physicists. My very presence in this land is confirmation of my theory.'

Will sees the irony in this, and the tragedy. John Page, lauded in his youth as a high achiever, and in his adulthood as a great scientist, is now just one of the sorry figures languishing in the royal dungeon of Inlandia. Marginalised, disreputable, spurned. What he and his fellow inmates have in common is how far they've fallen.

'There is good news, though, for the wretches,' John says. 'In Inlandia, potions and dusts have no effect. Sooner or later, everyone here loses the taste for anything other than healthy food and water. Even the least well visitor quickly bounces back to full health. It's part of the magic of the place.'

Will's mind swims with the wonder and the danger of it all. And then he remembers someone important.

'A man followed us here. I'm pretty sure he's an Actuary I saw at Uncle Max's. I'd seen him before, too, at Sandstone.'

John ponders the timeline, does some mental arithmetic. His public lecture in the Masonic Hall was probably the last straw for the Chancellery and the Republic. The slow turning of bureaucratic wheels must've delayed the dispatch of the assassin, giving John time to escape inland. Smith probably followed John's trail. After that trail came to nothing – the Actuary was manifestly too reliable to enter Inlandia – he probably returned to Redcliffe to find Will.

'I expect he's waiting for me outside,' John says. 'Or for us.'

Father and son ponder this unhappy fact. Then Will breaks the silence.

'I hate to see you here. Surely mum will let you out.'

'That, unfortunately, is not sure at all. Over the centuries, many travellers have reached Inlandia. Most new arrivals are dangerous in some way. And I'm the most dangerous of them all.'

## 19

# A BRIEF HISTORY OF NOW

The Teacher is very old. Louis De Rougemont met him in 1855. Afterward, in his memoir, he described him as a guru and medicine man who wielded a paranormal power over snakes. De Rougemont wrote admiringly of the Teacher's hair, tied in a unique feathery top-knot. Also his gecko tattoo. And his stripy long-johns.

Wizened and fidgety, the Teacher wears those same long-johns today. And the same hairstyle, though his top-knot is more a fore-knot on account of his hunched posture. He smells pleasantly of anise and Spanish brandy.

'Well, well, well,' he says fussily. 'Greetings Prince and welcome to Mkdos. We don't get many visitors anymore. And most of those who do come are fools and scoundrels. Drifters, stowaways, escaped convicts, young lovers on the lam. Getting here is no mean feat. There are rules, you see, about entering this kingdom. The place must be approached in the right way. A way that is circuitous. Full of deviations and setbacks. All this I'm sure you know. I suppose you also want to know about me, and the history of this place.'

The Teacher doesn't wait for Will's reply.

'My name was Gil Eannes. Now, though, people call me

Teacher. Other names, too. Nestor. The Apothecary. The Wetherman. I'm not sure they know what to call me,' he says through laughter.

'I've lived in Inlandia a very long time. Since 1518 on the old Outland calendar. Once Nicolaus Copernicus confirmed the world was round – and after Albrecht Dürer drew the spherical globe in accurate perspective – there was a fabulous rush of seafaring. All the great continents and islands of the New World were discovered. The Americas, Australia, Antarctica. Java le Grande, Tierra del Fuego, the Solomons and Tahiti. No longer was there nothing new under the sun. With João Vaz Corteral I sailed from Portugal aboard the *Rodrigues*, a mahogany caravel. Our minds were unwritten and capable of enormous designs. We would pursue a magnificent and impossible mission. Sailing to the antipodes. The ends of the earth.

'When we reached the southern coast of *Terra Australis* we sent our scouts far inland. They returned with beguiling reports of gold and gulls. And they relayed a native legend that spoke of a vast freshwater lake, which the local people called Wingilpin. On the strength of this news, I travelled to the interior. When I found the lake – really a sea – I decided to stay. Near the water, you understand, and the gold. When I arrived, the great pyramid was already here, already ancient. Since settling in Inlandia I've enjoyed miraculous health. The Mkdorii are naturally long-lived. Our roses fade but slowly. In principle, you can live forever here. The only causes of our ageing – the only limits to our lifespans – are the old assumptions and prejudices that people bring with them from the Outland. We have a leftover expectation that we will age, and so we do. But we don't have to.'

Will's head bulges with the Teacher's words – so amazing, so unbelievable – and with the spectacle of the Teacher himself – so unlike Mrs Crabbe of Ashburnham High.

'I've seen an abundance of marvels in my time here,' the

Teacher continues. 'And just as many disappointments. Wave upon wave of travellers have called on me. Eventually the Spanish and the Portuguese decided they were finished with this part of the world. Then came the French. Their kings and queens sent artists and poets. Men and women of culture and imagination. People with no words for "conformist" or "accountant" or "mass production". Then it was the turn of the Dutch. They sent merchants and adventurers, some of whom returned to the coast and eventually to Europe to tell of what they'd found. Then the English came. Not poets or adventurers but administrators. A dismal caste of surveyors and money-counters who arrived under a busy and bureaucratic flag. Apart from their flag, the bureaucrats brought their dim vision, their timidity, their ordinariness. When upstanding men like Sturt and Wentworth left the interior, they spread a thousand boring lies. They said the inland sea was a myth and there was no gold. The centre of the continent, according to these men, was a dead end. A null. As time went on, the bureaucrats installed themselves in positions of power. It was they who wrote the history of the continent. Earlier reports from the interior were discarded and discredited, shunted into the realm of myth. As the power of the Australian Republic grew, its leaders had less and less tolerance for people who strayed from the official view of history and Consistency. And yet the central civilisation lives on. A precarious existence, to be sure, and a hazardous one.

'Our people, you see, have split. Inlandia has turned on itself. The Outland culture is organised by race and class. Here, we separate by affiliation and creed. Members of the Queen's faction – the Athenians – take as their model the society of ancient Athens. They embrace Athenian culture and science. The wisdom of Aristotle and the medicine of Galen. Above all, they value learning and scholarship and the principles of law and good governance. But their rivals worship different gods. They look not to Athens but to Sparta, and they judge themselves on their strength, ruthlessness and prowess in battle. As you can well imagine, the politics and intrigues of Inlandia are diabolical. I try to stay out of them. I'm in touch with both factions but am tied to neither. The factions live different lives. They shop at different markets, send their children to different schools. They do mix, from time to time, at public events and in the corridors of the royal palace. Not very long ago, though, even that would've been inconceivable. The factions were on the brink of civil war. For the time being they maintain an uneasy truce. Uneasy, and probably temporary. Their beliefs and values are so different. They'll always have a natural hostility. But at this moment there's an even greater worry for both camps. The risk of invasion from outside Inlandia. The kingdom is alive with rumours of gathering armies and an imminent assault by the Republic and its servants. That danger is helping to keep the peace here. Naturally, the Spartans are eager to meet any invaders in battle.'

As usual, Will has a thousand questions. The Teacher's residence is a kind of elevated fort made from unribbed bamboo. Apart from the palace, the fort is the first Inlandian home that Will has seen from the inside. The Teacher lives very simply, with a pet minyip and a few pieces of furniture but little else. Noticing the absence of any kind of machine, Will asks about Inlandian technology.

The Teacher replies abruptly. 'We've heard about your "record players", your "computers", "electrical appliances". We've even seen some of them here, brought by Outlanders. We can't make them work. I doubt if they ever *could* work.'

He walks over to a primitive cupboard and returns with a crude brass chronometer, a mangled artefact brought by an early visitor to Inlandia.

'Take this little machine. Do you really believe it could tell time? Your father tried to give us electricity, just as others before him had tried. He promised to build a generator. The Mkdorii laughed. That kind of thing just doesn't work here. Much of the so-called science of the Outland is nonsense. We even have a word for it: Outlandish.'

From another cupboard the Teacher pulls out a papyrus scroll and begins to school Will on the strange alternative Inlandian science about record players (impossible) and skyscrapers (likewise); about sex and ageing; and about bunyips (which flourish throughout Inlandia), spiders (which are rare here) and butterflies (non-existent). All in all, Will is exposed to a rich body of lore and tradition that reminds him of Uncle Max's elaborate superstitions and house rules.

Though intrigued by the Mkdoan teachings, Will is sceptical of them. Could they really be true? He has seen with his own eyes the marvellous results of Republican science. Buildings towering usefully and safely. Mass transit networks of impressive complexity. All manner of electronic toys and tools and gadgets. And the Republic's greatest mechanical accomplishment, the Consistency Engine.

'Surely,' he says, 'there is some truth in the official science?'

'The Republic's truth? I've had enough of the Republic's truth,' the Teacher says bitterly. 'It weighs on us like a terrible burden.'

# 20

# AN UNEXPECTED VISITOR

AFTER WILL LEAVES the Teacher's bamboo fort, the royal guards escort him to his new quarters in the pyramid. An opulent, sprawling apartment fit for a prince. Narrow windows give a beautiful, panoramic view of the orchards and the vines and the lake below.

Jenny comes to check out her new master's new digs. She goes from room to room, running her hands over furniture and fittings and fabrics, almost skipping with joy. She has many reasons to be happy about her official attachment to the new prince. He is famous. He has shown kindness towards her. And she finds him and his story exotic and fascinating.

Will arranges for her to sleep in a small room nearby, and to eat and wash in the common areas used by the palace administrators and attendants.

'The Teacher is tutoring you on the ways of the Mkdorii,' she says. 'But I can tell you all the really useful things. The kinds of things he'll probably leave out, like the daily routine – and the daily bells. The first chimes each day sound the first watch. The next are at midday, then at the start of the night watch. We live our lives by the bells.'

She gives Will a handwritten schoolbook and he begins to read about Inlandia's guilds and occupations. Its chefs, artists, fishermen, engineers, plumbers, spearmen, pearl-divers, courtiers, booksellers, toysellers, conjurers, bunyip wranglers. And about how they live and where they came from – Europe, Asia, Tahiti, O-hawaii, plus many places whose names are now lost.

Will then reads another list, this one of Inlandian foods. Dugongs, rays, eels, catfish, goat, grapes, apples, eggs, jerky, damper, bush tucker and, in keeping with the Inlandians' partly seafaring origins, 'hardtack', also known as ships' biscuits.

Jenny refers Will to the chapter on Inlandia's lake and river fish. Carefully it lays out which ones are poisonous, and which ones are safe to eat – and delicious.

'The book doesn't say anything about ice-cream, but we love that, too,' she says. 'I make it all the time. Would you like me to make you some?'

Jenny is remarkable, Will thinks. Slight of build, even skinny, and yet she seems to view the world through a lens of food. He relishes her tutorials and her lists. The details of Inlandian culture are fascinating. But, for him, the lessons about Mkdoan politics are the most interesting, and important. He asks Jenny to share all she can about the Inlandian government and its palace intrigues.

'My father accepts the Queen's rule,' Jenny says, 'so long as the Spartans are shown public respect, and so long as my father is the Queen's viceroy and chief advisor.'

'Not a great set up,' Will says cautiously. 'Less like power sharing than power borrowing.'

'It's complicated. The factions tolerate each other most of the time, but each side knows that the other is always spying, always hatching plots.'

∞

Later that night, Will is in his apartment alone, taking notes from Jenny's schoolbook, when he hears a rhythmical knocking. Opening his door, he is amazed to see someone from the Outland. Someone he has known since primary school. Tim 'Loopy' Weston.

Will gives Tim an intense, fancy-meeting-you-here look. Tim's expression, though, is not one of surprise. It is his trademark grin.

The old friends shake hands, then bear-hug briefly. For Will, this is another awkward meeting with the friend who taught him about girls and fighting and much more besides.

'How'd you get in here, past the guards?'

'Told 'em I was with you.'

The Inlandian magic that transformed Will Page and Rani Sharma has had an even more drastic effect on Tim Weston. His Mkdoan incarnation is more confident, less wiry, more mature. If not for his punk-rock tattoos, he could pass for a senator or general from ancient Rome. To call this new version 'Loopy' would be absurd.

'How's your old man?' Tim asks, folding himself into the ivory settee next to Will's writing desk . 'Still minting his special brand of weirdness?'

'He's here, in the palace.'

Tim doesn't seem surprised by that, either.

'Oh,' he says, before recounting a version of his journey that is light on detail, light on explanation. Perhaps, Will thinks, he sees no need to justify his presence. Perhaps he thinks Will can work it out for himself.

As Tim speaks, Will follows a confounding train of thought.

During his trek inland with Rani, he was certain that it was the Actuary who was following them. Now, though, his certainty evaporates. Maybe he and Rani only *assumed* their shadow was the assassin. They never actually saw him during the trek. Will alone had seen him, and that was at Port Philip, and then at Uncle Max's house.

'They're staging an event for me,' Will says vaguely. 'Later this month, to welcome me to the kingdom. You should come. First I'll sort out a place for you to stay.'

Will summons a palace official and arranges for Tim to be billeted outside the pyramid with a family connected to the royal administration. After Tim leaves, Will sits thinking, looking out the window.

# 21

# RABBITS DON'T SURF

Tim Weston. What is he doing in Inlandia? He and Will had once been close. What happened to change that? Will's mind wanders back to the best days of their friendship. To the breathlessly hot summers when Loopy Weston and Rabbit Page rode their pushbikes down to the Loddon River on the southern outskirts of Redcliffe.

Rabbit had customised his clapped-out Malvern Star dragster into a pseudo BMX. Loopy's bike, though, was the real thing. Rabbit perhaps had the greater speed on bitumen, but Loopy came into his own once they reached the tracks leading down to the riverbank.

There, Loopy wrote the simple rules for their favourite game. At the deepest point in the river, the friends would swim to the bottom and carve messages on the decaying stump of an ancient gumtree. Rabbit called the stump Old Smoky, until Loopy said they should name it Trajan's Column.

The longer the message, the longer the boys had to hold their breath. According to the rules of the game, the first swimmer to resurface – nearly always Rabbit – had to buy minimum chips at Jan's Cafe on the way home. Newcomers

to the riverbank would gasp when the boys re-emerged –
boys who must surely have drowned minutes earlier. After
every dive, Loopy and Rabbit spread themselves out on the
bank, exhausted and exhilarated.

In winter the Loddon was the scene of a different spectacle. Every Sunday in July at three p.m. sharp, the water
corporation released a hundred million litres of turbid water
from Wombat Lake. The freed water organised itself into a
wave that raced past Redcliffe at an unnatural speed, only
petering out when it reached towns a hundred miles to the
north.

The locals called the flushing tea-coloured wave the
Bendigo Bombora. The bravest young men and women tried
to surf it on handmade Malibu boards. Riding the bendy
bommie was as much a rite of passage as a five-finger
discount at Lowe's Emporium, or pashing at Newstead
Lookout.

For two winters, Loopy watched the surfers and admired
their swagger. Part ballerino – half his ancestors were
dancers – he was never more eloquent than when describing
the surfers' downstream progress. Loopy Weston, bogan
poet.

It was only a matter of time before he challenged his
younger friend to ride the wave. One afternoon in the winter
holidays, he showed up at Will's place with two old wooden
boards. He didn't need to say anything else.

To prepare for this mad initiation, Will asked his father
about the Bombora. The professor replied with a detailed
description of the hydrology, topography and bathymetry of
the river and its bed. The more Will knew, the more he
worried.

He'd seen for himself the cold, foaming maw of churning
water that surged with terrifying speed from a place where,
only moments before, it had stagnated unwholesomely.

Despite these fears, though, Will bought a second-hand

wetsuit. When the day came to ride the bommie, he paddled with Loopy out to the midstream, all the while feeling like a water beetle about to be dunny-flushed. Maybe, he thought momentarily, he'd have had more confidence if his mother was still around.

At the critical moment, the debutantes took up their positions. A monstrous spumey wave appeared up-river. Bedsheet white and hyperventilating, Rabbit Page slid from his varnished board and swam down to Trajan's Column, grabbing hold of a gnarly root far below the foam-scum and backwash that squalled and moiled above.

To distract himself, he read the carved messages. Loopy's favourite girls and least favourite teachers. His best and dirtiest limericks. Each boy's plans for life and love.

Two fathoms above, Loopy rode the wave brilliantly on his first attempt – as he was always going to. Afterward he retrieved Will's abandoned board. The pair never spoke of the choke, but their eyes said everything and Will knew right away that their friendship could never again be as easy or as warm as it'd been during those beautiful, breathless summers.

22
___

# MUTINY

'How delightful to see you here,' Mary says when Will and his escort of royal guards arrive at the Queen's opulently furnished chamber. 'And how astonishing!'

Mary sends the guards away. Leading Will to a comfortable settee, she recounts for him the story of her journey to the interior.

'My expedition party set out full of hope and excitement. Hopelessly naïve in hindsight. We chose our route carefully but we were venturing into a vast and unforgiving wasteland, following in the tracks of earlier explorers – men I've told you about before, like Leichhardt and Coulthard and Horrocks – who'd died from dysentery and dehydration – and camels.

'Apart from these risks, we faced even greater dangers. The Republic made no secret that it opposed the venture. Questioning the Theory and the continent's official history amounted to heresy. And we all knew the Republic had ways to deal with heretics.

'I presumed at least one member of my party would be a Republican spy. Michael Smith was the most likely suspect.

He looked too comfortable in a business suit, and his flagrant normality made him the oddball in my band of eccentrics.

'Despite these dangers, we set out full of optimism. I had confidence in my men, despite their diverse backgrounds and mixed expertise. All of them seemed ambitious and driven, though their drivers were as different as their histories.

'For the first five hundred miles, talk of Lasseter's gold rather than scientific fame was what sustained us and glued us together. For the next five hundred, it was talk of gulls and an inland sea. When all these dreams came to nothing, we would've settled for a creek or a billabong or indeed any change in the landscape. But that was not to be.

'Where Louis de Rougemont had reported seeing an abundance of wonders – lush forests, fertile valleys, giant turtles, twenty-foot-long snakes – we found only sand. Where Lasseter had claimed to have uncovered a vast golden lode, we found only impoverished rock.

'William Buckley had travelled through the same country. When he returned to civilisation, he wrote of wading in bunyip-infested swamps on the edge of a great body of water – said to be an ancient remnant of the Great Flood. Now, though, we found no water at all. Only the desolation of a never-ending desert.

'Every one of these contradictions threw my mind back to the Midwinter debate. To when I'd taken on the Vice Chancellor. I winced at the memory.

'I wasn't the only one to be dogged by painful thoughts. For each of my men, early optimism had long since given way to fear and doubt.

'The heat wore us down. The weather conspired with the terrain to repel us, just as the weather and terrain had done for prior expeditioners. The sandy and stony ground seemed to have its own plans, one of which was to build our despair. From time to time, the landscape dangled hope. In every case, though, the hope turned out to be a mirage, a ruse. The country, it seemed, was determined to defeat us.

'Extremes of temperature made travel inefficient. There were few good times to walk each day. The horses died early in the expedition, as did any sense of goodwill or common purpose among my crew.

'They bickered and grew impatient with each other's quirks. Drayton spoke too much, Noakes not enough. Zouche made a flamboyant mess when he ate, while Smith's precise and ordinary habits were just as irritating.

'I thought I could trust Noakes, the head porter. I stayed close to him. But I knew, sooner or later, that my ragbag party would mutiny.

'Every day, the men sloughed off another layer of hope. Their jokes and banter became cruder, their glances more malevolent. In the men's eyes I'd ceased to be a leader, but they'd not yet decided what role I would play next.

'The options were many. I could've become food, just as the horses had. Or ballast, like much of our expensive equipment. Or, as the female captain of an otherwise all-male party, something much more frightening.

'Terrible, debilitating uncertainties hung over us all. When would the mutiny start? What form would it take? Who would lead it?

'In the end, the end came quickly. I caught Drayton whispering to two junior porters. Then Zouche fought with Smith and tried to strangle him. Or was it the other way round? During the tussle it was hard to tell.

'Next morning, though, things were somewhat clearer. The porters found Zouche dead, his throat neatly cut, and no sign of Smith.

'I'd been right about him. He was definitely a spy. He was also a calculating assassin. And I think his calculation was this. He would stay with us until we'd covered more distance than we could tolerate covering again. Until, that is, in every direction there were no stations or settlements, no feasible prospects of help or water.

'When we reached that point, all discipline had gone, as had our quadrants, seismographs, radios and balloons. This was the moment Smith chose to sow chaos and abandon us.

'After Zouche's death and Smith's disappearance, the expedition disintegrated. I experienced its last moments as a desperate sequence of still pictures. The maps and journals suddenly on fire. Drayton striking Noakes full in the face with a mattock. The junior porters running off to the east. Drayton grabbing my wrists.

'Then darkness when a cornsack covered my head. Just before oblivion took over, my last thoughts were of you.'

Mary pauses, then says candidly, 'I wonder why.'


∞


Will's mother describes how the porters saved her, and how, after Michael Smith left the party, the exhausted and delirious travellers were able to enter Inlandia.

That is how she came upon this rich and complex civilisation, the vivid, living proof of all her work on alternative histories. Once she'd learnt a little about the Mkdorii, everything fell into place. The hints in Outland history books. The surprising finds, such as the Mahogany Ship near Warrnambool and the Bellarine Keys near Geelong. Clearly, Australia was occupied and settled by Europeans long before Captain Cook and Arthur Phillip. The Republican history was a lie – just as she'd always suspected.

The Inlandians welcomed Mary with open arms, even treated her like Mkdoan royalty. Which, in fact, she was. Her ancestors were already celebrated, even idolised, as founding fathers of Inlandia.

In her physically enhanced form, Mary soon became Queen by law as well as on account of her genes.

The remnants of her expedition party were one of the biggest additions to Inlandia's population in many years – ever since Leichhardt and his men and livestock had arrived, for Inlandia was the solution to that mystery as well. The survivors from Mary's party moved into positions of power in the government and the royal court, just as Leichardt's had.

Sitting on the Queens' settee, Will feels a well of pride and happiness for his mother – owing to her spectacular validation as a scholar and her unexpected elevation as a monarch. But he feels, too, a strange disappointment. His mother has prospered so stunningly without her husband or son at her side.

'I did try to leave Inlandia,' she says, sensing Will's mixed feelings. 'More than once. Having arrived here, though, no-one can escape. No matter how hard they try. And no matter who or what they've left outside. I did miss you. Of course I did. And your father, too.'

'Then why's he in the dungeon?'

'I put him there. Partly for his safety, partly for mine. The kingdom is a restless, conspiratorial place.'

Though she doesn't say so, Mary's feelings about John Page are decidedly mixed. She has been apart from him nearly as long as they were together. And their marriage was, at least in her mind, a fragile one. Their different obsessions pulled them in diametric directions.

In Inlandia, before she became Queen, Mary dropped 'Page' from her name. Now, as Queen, she is pursued by other people. She knows, above all, that Lord Krull wants her for himself.

That interest is flattering but also dangerous. Ruthless Krull struggles to contain his most basic instincts. Peace in Inlandia, though, depends upon the Athenian–Spartan truce, which in turn depends on Mary and Krull getting along.

Will detects the chieftain's presence in his mother's thoughts.

'It must be difficult with Krull around,' he says.

'I've known him for a long time. Even before Inlandia.'

Will is stunned.

'Lord Krull wasn't always a Spartan chief,' Mary says. 'Once upon a time he was plain, ordinary Mr Noakes, my lead porter. That, though, was before he found his inner warrior.'

# 23

# THE POINT OF NO RETURN

AFTER WILL'S visit with the Queen, he goes in search of Rani.

'I've been exploring the village,' she says when he finds her sitting on the grass, cross-legged next to a fountain in the palace gardens. 'Such a delightful place.'

'It is,' Will answers, 'but flimsy, too.'

He shares with Rani his father's theories and fears; how Inlandia's existence depends on a miraculously fragile anomaly, and how, as an adult arrival and a recently respectable scientist, John Page poses a mortal threat – especially as he arrived in Inlandia as much by deliberate method as by happenstance.

'If, on purpose or by accident, my father convinces the Inlandians that the Outland reality is pre-eminent, and their own existence is little more than a colossal historical hiccup, then the coastal dictatorship might prevail. And every citizen of Inlandia would disappear in an instant.'

From the lakeside, Will and Rani watch the turtle riders, the crayfishermen, the frolicking bunyips and the breaching dugongs. The bunyips move in a strange stop-start manner, at once playful and furtive.

During the journey inland, Will stole glimpses here and

there of Rani – usually when she was washing or preparing for bed. A hint of the profile of her athletic hips and narrow waist. A glance at the flamingo-birthmark between her shoulder-blades. A flash of the cottony fabric of her sleep shorts. All these glimpses left permanent images in Will's mind – images he recalls whenever he can.

Rani watched Will sometimes, too, or at least Will suspected as much – and that idea, too, had been a subject of wonder for him. Rani's preferred dress in Inlandia is a colourful sari that shows off her hourglass shape, a shape newly enhanced by the magic of Mkdos. For Will now, Rani's sari and shape are further sources of delight.

That delight, though, is mixed with more complicated feelings. For several reasons, Will has told himself not to go all in with Rani. Not to fall head over his thickened heels. He remembers, for one thing, his long preoccupation with Laura Macdonald. And his brief ill-fated affair with the Murnanian floozy. After that sorry episode, he vowed not to fall in love too quickly, too emphatically.

There are other reasons, too, for Will to hold back. His parents' marriage is one. The Republic is another. The government would frown upon a match between a professor's son and a recently arrived migrant worker, no matter how bright and beautiful she is, and no matter how far the professor has fallen. There are rules about such things.

But then, Will thinks, those stupid rules don't apply anymore, now that he and Rani are in Inlandia. And he knows his feelings for Rani are deepening. Enchanting feelings that he probably couldn't hold back, even if he wanted to.

As Will and Rani walk along the waterfront, their arms brush together and they hold hands for the first time. After this, Will and Rani take regular evening walks to the lakeside – she in her sari, he in the loose Socratic robes of an

Athenian prince. Each time they meet, they hold hands more easily and with greater affection.

On their third walk, illuminated by bright stars and the lighthouse, Will and Rani notice something remarkable. In Inlandia, there is no moon.

And on that same walk, something almost as striking happens. For the first time since they left Redcliffe, Will and Rani stroll in a fine, misty, evanescent rain.

∞

It is one week from the royal reception and the pair are again spending time together, exploring the wonders of Inlandia.

As the afternoon turns into evening, Will and Rani walk down to the lighthouse and the waterfront. They pass groves of branching candlenuts. Bees graze on beds of swaying foxgloves and kangaroo paw. Inlandians – some of them pushing large babies in prams made from chunky logs – greet the Outlanders in diverse accents and with diverse vocabularies. Words from Welsh, Patagonian, Chinese, Dutch, Urdu and several tongues that are extinct outside this land.

Will and Rani play a private game of naming words adopted into English from other languages.

'Wunderbar.'

'Meringue.'

'Boomerang.'

'Sayonara.'

'Now we sound like Inlandians,' Will says.

Rani shares a story she once heard, about how the world's peoples are unexpectedly connected.

'The European and Indian languages have been traced back to a single ice-age dialect. The great works of English literature are not as foreign to me as you might think.'

Now the game is to find common words from that ice-age tongue that are still shared and intelligible today, in lands as distant as northern Britain and southern India.

Rani kicks off.

'*Ma* for mother and *pa* for father.'

'Good one,' Will says, before wracking his brain for other examples from the few foreign words he knows.

'There must be a word that links 'water' and *agua*,' he eventually says. 'Maybe something like *oo-a?*'

'I'll buy that. And how about *pisc* or *pish* for fish? The Latin word is *piscis*, as in Pisces, the star sign.'

The pair continue back and forth in this fashion, searching for primal names for animals and plants, the planets and the seasons.

Rani wins the game with a beautiful ancient word.

'Autumn comes from *autu*. It means "change".'

So much, Will thinks, for the legend of Babel.

On the beach, another game is underway: an archery competition, lit by burning torches. The competitors use bows and arrows of a unique Mkdoan design. The loosed arrows make a charmed sound as they fly through the balmy air. Each projectile leaves behind a faintly luminescent trail that reminds Will of the sparks he sees behind his eyelids whenever he glances too long at the sun. Or perhaps the trails are more like the ones left by the sparklers he played with as a child at Redcliffe's Oktoberfest.

As the pair pass by, an archer beckons to Rani and offers her a bow. After some brief words of instruction, Rani steps up to take part.

And she is a natural. As soon as she takes the bow in her hands, Will can see the connection she has with the curved structure, inlaid with mother-of-pearl and strengthened by a sinewy cord Will later learns is thousand-year-old bunyip gut.

Will watches as Rani notches an arrow, drawing it back so that the fletching – perhaps emu feathers – gently caresses her lips before sliding gently down her cheek to rest neatly below her right jawline. Following the line of the arrow with her eye, Rani shifts her focus from the slightly bulbous arrowhead to the target at the end of the flight.

The moment Rani releases the arrow, it's as though she is no longer there. As the missile arcs high above the sand, she flickers in Will's vision. For the briefest of moments he has the sensation that he has blinked and kept sight of his surroundings but not of Rani. Quickly he double checks to make sure she is really here.

Whistling a melodic warble as it goes, the arrow streaks down-field. When it thuds into the target it throws out a splash of colour and sparks. In the sound, Will hears a visceral longing, a sort of cry that is not so much mournful as hopeful. It is a sound he feels as much as hears.

As the arrow strikes, Rani lowers the bow and dips her head in reverence. Then she turns to face Will, a broad smile on her face, tears in her eyes.

'Oh, Will. I've never felt such stillness. Such belonging.'

Will can't be sure but Rani seems more a part of the world now than she did before. Had she grown even taller? More statuesque? More beautiful?

Will shakes his head, unsure where to look. For some reason, he can't meet her gaze. Instead his eyes fall on the small Athenian tiara she has taken to wearing – an attempt to replace a recent loss. It shimmers in the afternoon light, reminding Will of the waters of the inland sea.

Rani smiles.

'I feel like Lord Rama with his mighty bow. My mother always asked me to be kind, like the Lady Sita. To be dutiful and compassionate. But she also wanted me to find my own strength. That's what this feels like to me.'

In the days that follow, whenever Will is looking for Rani he knows he'll find her at the archery range. There, she surrounds herself with a cadre of young archers. They teach her about technique and the principles of their sport. She instructs them in compassion and tradition and inner strength.

After each drill session, Rani and her troop gather under the shade of a giant gingko tree to share stories. Rani often selects from the great Hindu epic, the *Ramayana*. Inspired, others recite ballads and sagas from their own cultures. In a curious way the stories meld together as the group adapts them to the legends and politics of Inlandia. They are building nothing less than a new Mkdoan mythology.

The group of archer-authors swiftly gain a reputation for their flair and creativity, standing out for their adoption of colourful silk saris and lungis in preference to more traditional Mkdoan garments.

One archer, a Spartan youth with broad shoulders and a straight back, approaches Rani during an afternoon of practice and speaks in hushed tones.

'*Duyfken*, why do you look away once a shot has been made? Surely, where the arrow ends up is where your attention should go?'

As Rani draws another arrow from the quiver at her hip, she smiles at the name her followers have given her.

'Everything is in the preparation of the shot. Whether it strikes true or not is no longer in my control. Once loosed, there is no return. No going back.'

## 24

## A DANGEROUS BOAST

Every Inlandian of note attends Prince William's royal reception – Athenians and Spartans alike. The invitees gather in the foyer of the great pyramid of Quincampoix, then form themselves into a grand procession. Mary Page, Will Page and Rani Sharma lead the procession into the Great Hall at the pyramid's heart.

Sandstone University has its own Great Hall, really just an oversized lecture theatre. The Great Hall at Quincampoix couldn't be more different: an enormous, rectangular, golden box lit by ponderous lamps. Something like a massive mead-hall in the longhouse of super-rich Vikings.

Mary Page sits on a high timber platform at the end of the Hall. The High Queen of Inlandia.

The Grand Geographer of Mkdos is Master of Ceremonies. Wearing a stately gown of purple velvet trimmed with kangaroo, he stands below the Queen's platform. From that position, his job is to formally welcome the VIPs, and to announce the major stages of the reception: the dinner courses and the commencement of dancing.

A stickler for protocol, he begins by paying tribute to the founders and champions of Inlandia, whose names he reels off. Lasseter, de Rougemont, de Groote, La Perouse, Buckley, Heidegger.

*Everyone has their heroes*, Will thinks to himself.

Then the Geographer names the honoured guest. This brings cheers and applause, especially from the rustic table that the guest shares with Rani, Jenny and Tim.

Prince William blushes.

Rani is pleased for Will to be surrounded by friends. All the guests are pleased to be surrounded by mountains of food. Chicken, stingray, trout, haggis, damper, pigeon pie, ice-cream. The smorgasbord is Jenny's favourite list.

The chefs of Mkdos have been busy, and so have its artists and artisans. The foremost members of the many Inlandian guilds had rushed to make masterpieces for the event. Fili-greed silverware from Elizabethtowne. Tapestries from the hamlet of Shrewsbury. Paintings and fine marble sculptures from Penhadigon. These and other artworks now line the hall. Together, they form a spectacular multi-media fresco that tells the story of Inlandia's history.

Will, though, is almost too distracted to notice the artworks and the story they tell. He is overwhelmed with stimulus, with memories, and with strange trains of thought.

The food, the beer, the dancefloor, the maids, the atmosphere – the whole thing reminds him of Redcliffe's chaotic Oktoberfest. And he notices how Tim Weston, formerly of Redcliffe, is the life of the party.

As the night wears on, Tim drinks more and more of the free beer and tells more and more fanciful stories of his life and adventures. Stories of how he surfed twenty-foot waves, collected dozens of tattoos, and, at Sandstone, won all the races in the Janitorial Olympics.

Noticing how Rani listens, hanging on every word, Will becomes ever more worried that Tim will mention the Bendigo Bombora – and Will's choke. And then Rani will know about it.

As though aware of that fear, Tim dances around the subject in a playfully tormenting way. Or, at least, that's what Will thinks he's doing – by emphasising words like *swimming* and *waves* and *courage*, and by describing how he saw a *little mouse* when he visited Will in the palace.

Throughout their friendship, Tim has always been several steps ahead on the journey towards girls and women. Now, in his beer-fuelled banter, he parades his sophistication by throwing around euphemisms and innuendoes such as *little deaths* and *little guns*.

Prompted in this way, Will touches the miniature pistol that is tucked deep inside his robes. Thanks to the magic of Inlandia, the weapon has transformed into a small cannon, which Will can still hold comfortably in his palm. He likes to handle it and to keep it close by.

Tim hazards a drunken guess at what Will is doing.

'Stop fingering your pocket rocket,' he says. 'I've got one, too, don't you know?'

This brings laughter from everyone. Everyone except Will, who fears that, any minute, Tim will ask Rani to dance. And, even worse, that she will accept. He imagines what he'll do if that happens. Cut in. Or, better still, call over a few Royal guards and denounce the new arrival as a Republican spy. For that, Will reasons, is surely what Tim is.

With such thoughts occupying Will's mind, he sits silently and sullenly while the conversation ranges widely around him. Outland and inland. Athenians and Spartans. Bunyips and minyips. All these are debated and evaluated, as are Inlandia's institutions and customs and fears. As the reception begins to peter out, the talk turns to Inlandia's isolation – and whether it's possible to leave.

'No one has ever left,' Jenny says sleepily. 'But I've heard there are theories about ways out. I've also heard many people have tried to leave, and have died in the attempt.'

'I reckon,' Tim says, 'that only the *bravest*, most deter-mined person could do it.'

Will knows Tim's strengths and weaknesses. How fast he can run and how long he can hold his breath. Tim won most of their childhood contests, excelling in feats of strength and agility. Will knows, too, that Tim's prowess has only grown in Inlandia. But he will not be bested this time, and especially not in front of Rani.

Will feels emboldened by his epic journey to the interior. And the Inlandian magic makes him feel braver still. He doesn't like how Tim looks at Rani or how she looks at him. Deep in his stomach he feels a bubble of jealousy about his old friend and new rival.

The bubble explodes in a burst of bravado. Seated on an ancient wooden bench, inside an ancient golden pyramid, surrounded by guests attending a grand to-do in his honour, Will voices boldly and with false assurance a fatal sentence.

'I know the way out.'

# 25

# A PARTING OF WAYS

THE NEXT MORNING, in the cool light of day, Rani and Jenny are with Will in the palace gardens when they realise he is serious about leaving. Jenny immediately insists on going with him. Rani insists on staying behind.

'I'm appreciated here,' Rani says. 'That's why I could pass into Inlandia. Because, in the Outland, brown-skinned foreigners are ignored. And there's so much good I can do here, as an associate of the royal household, to help unify Mkdoan society. I can also keep an eye on your father in the dungeon.'

Will ponders Rani's explanation for why she could enter Inlandia. He has his own theory, that she possesses royal or divine blood, which resonates somehow with the Mkdoan magic. But the point is moot. Rani isn't coming.

'For you,' she says, 'Inlandia fulfilled the dream of finding your parents. For me, it realised a different dream. The dream of migration, the dream that brought my family to Australia in the first place. Finally, I've arrived in a beautiful green land in which I'm valued and can do purposeful work. I've fulfilled the greatest wish of my mother and father.

Inlandia is the paradise they sought all along. I feel as though, by staying here, I'm breaking my pledge to you. But I know for sure that your journey will succeed, and that we'll meet again soon.'

Holding Rani to her pledge had never occurred to Will. To him, it is no longer binding or even relevant. She'd brought him safely to the interior. He feels, now, that she is more a partner than a protector. And privately he hopes that, one day soon, they might make a different kind of pledge to each other – whatever the Outland society thinks about that.

Will and Rani both shed tears before they part. Farewelling the Queen and John Page is also difficult. Neither of Will's parents can understand why he would want to leave, or whether in actual fact he *can* leave. And, if so, how long he'll be away. They both warn him to be careful. And John warns him, in particular, to watch out for the Actuary who might be lurking just beyond Inlandia's borders.

When Will farewells Tim, he considers warning him off Rani but thinks better of it. Rani has Will's trust, even if Loopy doesn't. After that and other goodbyes, Will fills his old backpack with provisions along with a handful of gold Inlandian doubloons, just in case he needs them. As he carefully wraps the precious family photo and its intricate silver frame in a scrap of bulrush papyrus, he almost changes his mind. He has come so far. How could he turn away from his newly reunited family on what amounts to little more than an unspoken dare?

But he is resolute. After changing into his Outlander clothes, he walks stoically from his apartment and the palace. When he meets Jenny she makes fun of his now ill-fitting blue-jeans and polo shirt, suitable neither for Spartan battle nor Athenian contemplation.

'Where should we start?' Jenny asks.

'Rani and I arrived in Inlandia just beyond the river, east of Quincampoix. That must be the boundary. I think we should start there.'

As Jenny crosses the river – carefully, at the shallowest point, holding Will's hand the whole way – she remembers being thrown in by her father. Will's thoughts, too, go momentarily to that day.

Once on dry land, Will and Jenny begin to walk to and fro among the ankle-high yellow flowers, feeling for changes in themselves and in the world around them. Hidden doorways. Stronger or weaker gravity. Heavier or lighter air. Gaps or burs in existence. They scan the ground for signs of desert, and for any other hint that they are on the right track.

No matter how they search, though, Will and Jenny find no trace of the Outland. In more and more elaborate ways, their hopes come to nothing, their paths just twist back on themselves.

Re-crossing the river and returning to the outskirts of Quincampoix, Will and Jenny call on the Teacher. Maybe he knows the way out.

∞

'No one has ever left Inlandia,' the Teacher says, stroking the minyip that has curled up asleep on his lap. 'Except by dying.'

'Surely you must know something,' Will urges. 'Something that can help us.'

The Teacher shuffles in his seat, waking the minyip who gives Will a foggy but meaningful glance. The Teacher frowns, then begins to speak in a hushed, conspiratorial tone.

'In the century after Inlandia became closed to the world, a cult believed escape was possible. Members of the cult idolised the sixteenth-century scientist-philosopher, Sir

Francis Bacon. They accepted every kind of mad heresy. The Hollow Earth Theory. Ancient aliens. Incompletism. And the idea that Bacon had secretly authored Shakespeare's poems and plays. The cult is rumoured to have had other strange beliefs, too, about early exploration and the shape of the world. They whispered that Earth was not always a sphere; that the East and West Indies were once the same place; that Columbus was right when he thought the eastern islands of the Americas were the eastern islands of Asia. Within the cult there were countless debates and sub-heresies about the precise shape of the world. The cultists knew Columbus himself had held provocative views. He was sure the world wasn't spherical but pear-shaped. And on the pear's nipple sat Eden, or Valhalla, or Mount Olympus – at least that's what he thought. Some of the cultists maintained even stranger beliefs. According to one branch of heresy, the world was originally a narrow cylinder. Others favoured a helix or a corkscrew. Yet others a heart, a doughnut or an hourglass. The cultists blamed Copernicus for taking the fun from these speculations. Another secret was also whispered. The cultists maintained that an outward route connected Inlandia to the rest of the continent. They spoke of a hidden path leading from the Northern Crags, beyond the Motoporo Forest. But I urge you to drop your quest, young Will. Even exploring that region is desperately dangerous. Its connection to the world holds secrets even more ancient than Inlandia.

'I know you'll hold fast to your plans, and probably won't take this advice, but I implore you. Stay here with us and share our life and our fate. I've met your father, heard some of his ideas. He's on the right track, that is certain. But there's much he doesn't understand. Other cultures have glimpsed the very same truths he's grappling with. Those cultures used words like dust and magic and miracles to describe the same thing. All these phenomena, though, are almost certainly symptoms of a deeper truth. I know your intentions are noble, and that you are armed with your father's theories. But don't put too much store in them. They're not worth dying for.'

**26**

———

# A DEAD END

With Jenny still in tow, Will sets out immediately for the forest and, a few miles beyond, the boggy terrain that is the not-very-welcoming doormat of the Northern Crags. Inlandia's badlands. The Teacher was right when he said Will wouldn't follow his advice.

Using Jenny's local knowledge, the companions find a way through the foul-smelling bogs to the equally obnoxious Crags. As soon as they enter the rocky zone, a morbid gloom envelops them. Sulphurous vapours rise from volcanic fissures. The sun struggles to shine through the permanently charcoal cloud-cap.

The outer perimeter of the Crags is a vast semi-circular cliff, as sheer as it is tall. Along barren slopes and round spiking tors – cold in the day and freezing at night – the travellers scramble over rock falls and a bed of broken slate, probing for a way through the great crescent-shaped barrier.

In this gruelling fashion, Will and Jenny make their search for an uncertain goal. Perhaps a tunnel, or a staircase carved by ancient hands in the fierce rock. Perhaps a narrow pass, invisible from a distance, but opening out into the land beyond.

Time after time, Will and Jenny come to a dead end at the looming cliff face and must retrace their steps, back into the forbidding, shadowless maze. Following curling paths for many days, Will and Jenny become hopelessly lost.

There is no escape outward from the labyrinth, but there is no apparent way back, either. (The pair have left no trail of signs or string or crumbs.) No way to return to their families and – foremost in Will's thoughts – to Rani.

Will and Jenny now know why so many people perished trying to leave Inlandia. And the companions see direct evidence of their predecessors' fate. Every kilometre or so, Will and Jenny come upon a human skeleton, picked clean and partially scattered by scavengers and vermin. These discoveries add to the feeling of utter hopelessness.

In the depths of this predicament, Jenny feels an urge to confess.

'Not long after you arrived in Inlandia,' she says, 'my father ordered me to spy on you and report back. He told me to keep lists and pay close attention to everything you did. Every word, every habit, every gesture, big or small. Your father is to blame, really. He used to be a major somebody in the Outland. That's why no one trusts him here. And that's why lots of people are suspicious of you, too. Guilt by association, if you know what I mean. But I'm sorry for spying on you. It means nothing now, but I would never have told my father anything really important – anything about you or Rani or your family. Lord Krull is a terrible father. And I'm more a part of your world now than his. I'd rather not go back to him at all.

'There's more, too. Lord Krull has spies in the palace. They even spy on the Queen in her bathing chamber and dressing closet. My father receives the spies' reports with much interest. Spartan women wear rough underclothes or none at all. Apparently the Queen, though, wears all sorts of fancy things under her royal gowns.'

Jenny is right about Krull's interest in the spies' reports. Spartan women think nothing of wrestling outdoors, naked. Even their everyday dress leaves nothing to the imagination. Krull, though, prefers it when his primitive imagination has work to do.

Krull's interest in the Queen has another spice to it as well. In the Outland, a porter would never be allowed to match up romantically with a scholar. In the pursuit of someone like Mary Page, Mr Noakes could never have been a contender. In his Inlandian form, however, he is now playing in an altogether different league and to a whole new set of rules.

Will listens carefully to Jenny's confession. He notices she has an odd, third-hand understanding of what the Outland must be like. Probably all children born in Inlandia do, he thinks.

He notices in her, too, a peculiar and endearing naiveté. He had brought her along so he could share with her the wonders of the outland. But the journey is turning out to be dangerous, and probably hopeless. In retrospect he would rather she had stayed with her family. And yet, in the worst moments, her attachment is a comfort, her company priceless. Will feels immensely proud of the waifish ward who never complains, never shows any fear.

'There is nothing for you to apologise about,' he says. 'I know you meant no harm and would never have betrayed me.'

Trapped and lost, foundering in despair, Will and Jenny make camp as best they can under a great shoulder of rock. Then they fall asleep, their bodies exhausted, their dreams troubled.

∞

When Will awakens into the oppressive half-light, he notices immediately that a third person has joined their camp. A mysterious boy, perhaps fourteen years old and vaguely familiar.

Jenny is soon awake, too, and regarding the boy with wide eyes. The boy helps Will and Jenny to their feet and gives them water and food. The food isn't in any of Jenny's lists or the Inlandian books she has shown Will during his unofficial induction. It's a kind of Outlander cake.

The new arrival is normal looking, physically sound, even slightly handsome. Will, though, plays a mental game with the boy's features, extending and magnifying each one of their little flaws and imagining what he would look like if all the adjustments were carried to their extremes.

The boy, Will thinks, would look monstrous. And then he knows.

'Hello Grig,' he says, to the boy he first met in the Tannahill basement.

'Follow me,' Grig says.

He leads Will and Jenny a short distance – it feels like no more than twenty yards or so – and shows them the concealed entrance to a tunnel. The entrance to the Under-world. The way to the Outland.

# 27

## A BREATH IN THE DARKNESS

WILL and Jenny had searched for Inlandia's front gate. Grig, though, shows them the back door. As Grig leads the way through the deep and narrow tunnels of the Underworld, Will keeps comparing them, unfavourably, to the passageways beneath Sandstone University. Much less hospitable. Much more dangerous.

Though Grig carries a small lantern, the way is still deathly dark. Moisture trickles down the unstable walls and drips from the unstable ceiling. Every now and then, the travellers hear rocks collapsing behind them – dashing any hopes they might've had of using this route to return to Inlandia.

Grig says few words, speaking only when necessary to guide his companions over the loosest rocks or past the steepest drops. He travels through the perilous tunnel with such confidence that Will thinks he must've come this way, or a similar one, several times before. Perhaps he's the only living being who can shuttle back and forth between Inlandia and the Outland.

After maybe five kilometres of tight twists and narrow turns, the tunnel opens out into a long cavern. The cavern has a wide flat floor and a high vaulted ceiling. A chasm – roughly rectangular, about a hundred yards long and forty yards wide – stretches along the right side of the cavern. Gingerly Will peers over the edge. The chasm's depth, it seems, is infinite.

A transparent wall serves as the outer boundary of the abyss. Perhaps a metre thick, the wall consists of a kind of mineral crystal or natural glass. Beyond the wall, thousands of min-mins float in a vast starry void. The gathered souls of the dead.

Bubbles and flaws occlude the crystal, but the travellers can still see through and out into the void beyond. The souls' predominant movement is outward. They are drawn to the timeless infinity of nothingness that spreads out beyond the wall. But they are fascinated, too, by the wall itself, and by the cavern and the lip of the abyss. And especially by the passing humans and their beckoning lantern.

Entranced, a few of the souls drift closer to the glass. To catch more souls' attention, Will and Jenny begin to pitch pebbles at the barrier. Grig stands by with his lantern. The projectiles hit the crystal then fall into the abyss. A murmuration of souls approaches, and Will and Jenny throw more rocks.

When perhaps a dozen souls are just two or three man-lengths from the glass, Will can see their sketchy, pearlescent outlines: mere suggestions of spindly limbs and shimmering faces. The souls seem worried. And in a strange, oscillating manner, they appear to be trying to communicate. They appear, in fact, to be warning the travellers to be quiet.

Will, though, is blind to the warnings. Spellbound by the floating souls, he takes out his pocket cannon. Perhaps, he thinks, he can break the glass and free them.

He readies the weapon and fires a crazy-brave, marble-sized cannonball that ricochets off the crystal and makes an ear-splitting boom. The boom echoes back and forth along the cavern, broadcasting outward through the tunnel and downward into the abyss.

Now the three travellers are just as worried as the souls had been. The trio hold their breath and the cavern falls utterly silent. The silence hangs on valiantly until a frightening noise rises from the chasm. A noise like a giant washcloth being dragged across a huge square of sandpaper.

First one tentacle appears, then another, and another. The tentacles belong to a creature that has hauled itself up from the bottomless depths. A horrible, nameless, unfinished creature, larger than a bunyip and much stranger. Alien and sluglike, a thing outside nature, recklessly conjured aeons ago. Primeval. Teratological. Labyrinthodontal.

Catching Jenny with the tip of a tentacle, the monster coils a slimy arm around her, then takes her into itself in a horrifyingly fast and effortless way, as though she's a featherweight doll. She tries to scream but there's not enough time, not enough air. The only sound she can make is a brief, spasmy, blood-curdling whimper.

Will lunges at the monster but Grig seizes him with greater speed and drags him from the creature's reach.

'She's lost!' Grig shouts. 'We have to get out of here!'

Will, though, is paralysed with fear and grief.

Grig grabs Will around the shoulders and hustles him to the other end of the cavern, then onward into the northern tunnel.

The boys run in a delirium, pursued by something contemptuous of life, something older and more frightening than death.

When they reach what Grig judges to be a safe distance, he stops.

'Give me the cannon!' he shouts.

Taking the weapon and backtracking thirty yards or so, he selects what he thinks is the right spot, then fires again and again at the ceiling.

A throaty, burbling sound fills the tunnel as a grievous mass of writhing limbs rounds the nearest bend.

Grig continues his barrage until, finally, the little cannon-balls persuade tons of suspended rock to collapse and seal the passage. No one will ever use this route again. Jenny's worldly remains will be forever lost.

Now seemingly protected from the hideous creature, the boys continue on through the tunnel.

At its deepest point the tunnel disappears into an underground river. The only way forward is underwater.

Grig removes his pack, fills his lungs with air, then plunges into the dark water to check the current and feel for a passage. A minute or so later he resurfaces.

'We can make it,' he says.

Will hesitates.

'You have to trust me.'

Terrified, Will holds his breath – just as he did in the Loddon with Loopy and Trajan's Column – and plunges into the river.

The distance underwater is much longer than he expected, and swimming in the disorienting dark takes an alarmingly long time. When finally he emerges he is utterly spent. His lungs burn with pain.

Grig swims back to retrieve the boys' packs. Then he and Will rest before setting off again. After walking for an hour or so, the pair come to the end of the tunnel. Squinting in the sunlight, they are soon breathing the open air. The air of the desert. The air of the Outland.

# PART III

---

HORRORS AND MARVELS

# EXTRACTS FROM LOUIS DE ROUGEMONT'S DIARY

# INLAND SEA, 1854

I waded out to where the turtles were, and on catching a big six-hundred-pounder, I calmly sat astride his back. Away swam the startled creature, mostly a foot or so below the surface. When he dived deeper I sat far back on the shell, and then he was forced to come up. I steered my queer steed in a curious way. When I wanted my turtle to turn to the left, I simply thrust my foot into his right eye, and vice versa for the contrary direction. My two big toes placed simultaneously over both his optics caused a halt so abrupt as almost to unseat me.

# GULF COUNTRY, 1855

Just before the battle commenced I had real inspiration that practically decided the affair without any fighting at all. It occurred to me that if I mounted myself on stilts, some eighteen inches high, and shot an arrow or two from my bow, the enemy would turn tail and bolt. And so it turned out.

# 28

## A DEBT REPAID

As soon as Grig emerges from the Underworld, his eyes turn black, his skin turns clammy and he reverts to his monstrous, fish-like form. A few yards from the tunnel exit, he plonks himself down on the desert sand next to Will.

Jenny is lost and Will can't get that fact out of his mind. The fairy-like ice-cream girl he first saw in the mysterious photograph at Sandstone. She was his friend and ward and now she's dead. He failed her by taking her on a reckless quest that began with a stupid lying boast.

'I know you felt you owed me a debt,' Will says gravely. 'I know, too, that you couldn't have foreseen that Jenny would perish on the journey. But I wish you'd never taken us that way. I wish I'd stayed in Inlandia with Jenny and Rani. Consider your debt fulfilled, if ever you owed me one.'

'I did owe you, Will Page. Not for rescuing me from the Tannahills. I would've escaped from there, sooner or later. I would've killed them, sooner or later. I owe you nothing for that. But I owe you for treating me with respect. And I'll repay that debt now with some respectful advice. You're a fool to think you could've survived in Inlandia. You were almost certain to die in the Crags. You and Jenny both. And if by some miracle you made it back to the pyramid and the village by the lake, you'd soon be annihilated by the Republic's arrogant, creeping, devastating truth. Or, even sooner, by the Republic's army.'

'What army?' Will asks.

Grig points to the southern horizon, which is alive with movement. A vast column of soldiers, marching towards Inlandia. The Republic's secret weapon.

In the distant heat, the figures resemble the toy soldiers of a careless child. Broken, misshapen, melting.

'That army. The only way for you to save your Inlandian friends, and the only way for you to give meaning to Jenny's death, is to fight the Republic head on. You have to go to Port Phillip. You have to convince the Outlanders that Inlandia is real. Otherwise, you'll never see Rani or your parents again.'

Will mulls this over.

'I liked you more,' he says, 'when you had nothing to say.'

∞

After parting from Grig, Will embarks on the long journey back to Port Phillip and its jewel, Sandstone University.

The journey over deserts and plains is easier and safer in reverse. Will knows the way – and what hazards to avoid. Just as important, this time there is no sign of a follower, Actuary or otherwise, shadowing his progress.

But the journey still requires weeks of arduous walking. Will feels desperately lonely. On this journey, he can't swap stories with Rani or anyone else.

Just as he did before, he bounces over rocks and bushes in his mind. Every morning he uses Uncle Max's plastic tarp to collect desert dew for water. Instead of Max's pound-cake and lemon-butter bread, he grazes this time on Inlandian delicacies such as fishpaste and hardtack. *Very* hardtack, Will thinks.

In Inlandia, he got used to his new height and physique. His limbs were longer there and he'd grown muscles where he never expected to. Now, though, he is back to his old shape, and to walking on his original, stubbier, pre-Mkdoan legs.

When Will finally reaches the westernmost station of the eastern rail network, he is exhausted and dishevelled. With a shiny gold doubloon – a marvellous windfall for the sceptical stationmaster – he buys a ticket for the coast. After boarding the nearly empty train, he spreads out in an unoccupied carriage, savouring the luxury of travelling on wheels rather than on foot.

The few short hours of travel that follow are a time for Will to reflect. He may have regained his old legs, but he sees the world through new eyes. Will wonders. Did Buckley and de Rougemont feel the same way when they, too, returned from the inland to 'civilisation'? And had they felt the same fear?

Thanks to Inlandia, many of the mysteries of Will's life have now been solved. Possibly, too, some of the deepest mysteries of the universe. But a host of new uncertainties now confront him. One question is paramount. What will he do when he arrives at his destination? That question is soon urgent. He is back at Sandstone.

# 29

# THE CHALLENGE

Gothic-style colleges and chapels. Towering steeples and finials. Fine avenues and annexes.

Dull and unimaginative men built the university, but it still possesses an undeniable beauty.

Will arrives at the main campus late in the evening. Fliers posted on walls and pillars tell him he has arrived on an important date. The winter solstice. The day of the Midwinter Debate.

The Sandstone style of debating is a kind of improvised conversational chess. Each round, a contender puts forward a proposition, then seeks to prove it. The opponent's job is to quickly come up with a convincing, devastating rebuttal.

Will knows immediately what he must do. Via the supply-dock hatchway he is soon in the tunnels and inhaling the familiar smell of damp and rats – an odour that brings back pleasant memories of his school days, and painful memories of the claustrophobic Underworld.

Will follows the main passageway till he reaches the branch that leads to the stage of the Great Hall. In that noble chamber, the VC is speaking at the rostrum – until, that is, a trap-door opens in the middle of the stage. To the amazement of the VC and the audience, a scruffy, dusty, dishevelled-looking boy climbs out.

'I'm Will Page,' he says meekly, squinting, a rabbit in headlights. 'And I claim the right. . . I claim the right to debate Oliver Macdonald.'

The VC's mind races.

*I know this boy. I've seen him before. One of the truants who eavesdropped in the tunnel below my office.*

Macdonald knows, too, the other members of the Page family. They are central to his plans for the continent's interior. Privately he is happy for the boy to speak. Perhaps he will let slip some news about Tim Weston's mission. Perhaps he will reveal other secrets that are valuable to the Republic.

Publicly, the VC pretends that high-mindedness is why he will allow Will to speak.

'This truly is an open debate,' he says loftily, still at the rostrum. 'This boy has some connection to Sandstone. And, evidently, some knowledge of its tunnels. I invoke the Chairman's discretion. The boy is welcome to debate me. And, in front of all our esteemed friends, he is welcome to lose.'

The audience cheers.

Now it's the turn of Will's mind to race.

Over the past few months, he has encountered a whole new science and a whole new civilisation. In all his life he was never a confident debater, or even a very competent one. But now, thanks to his experiences in the interior, he possesses a vast reserve of novel material he can use against the VC. He only wishes he had more time to prepare.

Yet he knows he must do something this very moment. Grig was right. If Will chokes now, he'll break a promise to Inlandia. And Jenny's death will have been for nothing.

Technicians escort Will to a second microphone at the far left of the stage. Gingerly he clears his throat, then settles on what he thinks will be his strongest proposition.

'There's a civilisation,' he says, 'in the centre of Australia.

It's called Inlandia, or Mkdos. The people there ride turtles and wear Greek robes and tunics. They have bunyips, too, and a great pyramid of gold. More than one person from Sandstone has gone to Inlandia. My parents are there right at this moment. Tim Weston, too, who used to work here.'

The VC smiles a Cheshire Cat smile before responding dismissively, 'Tim *Loopy* Weston, don't you mean? A crazy, disreputable character. Just like the others. I thought this was going to be a serious debate, young Will. The audience and I have no time for such heretical nonsense. We've heard the same claims from your mother, at this very forum, and have shown them to be lies. Just to be sure, we monitor the inland with drones and agents. Let me say, once and for all, there is no lost civilisation in the interior. The inland is a vast, worthless desert, suitable only for strip mining and bomb tests.'

And just to be doubly sure, the VC has mobilised an army. A desert army, whose sole purpose is to find, enter and destroy Inlandia.

After receiving the Engine's advice about unreliable agents, the VC directed the Republic to assemble a unique force, in case he ever needed it. Port Phillip's prisons and asylums and reform schools were emptied of criminals, lunatics and degenerates – or at least that's what the Republicans call them.

The Republican Army put the new recruits through basic training, gave them weapons and escorted them to a gathering point in the central desert – the point where Grig and Will saw them after exiting the Underworld.

Will's first move in the debate has revealed a great deal. His mention of Inlandia, and particularly the presence of Loopy there, is an invaluable gift to Macdonald – the confirmation he hoped to receive.

The Republican spy, it seems, has crossed over. He has demonstrated that Inlandia can be penetrated, so long as the intruder is sufficiently unreliable. The Engine's intuition was correct. The VC gives a signal to Mallory, his right hand man. The signal is the order to unleash the Republic's mish-mash army. The order to invade.

Will doesn't notice the signal, and anyway he can't have known what it means. Having botched his opening gambit, he changes tack. He will share with the Outlanders some Inlandian science. Some of the teachings of the Teacher.

'Butterflies,' he says. 'How can they exist at all? Most birds eat insects. And most birds are larger, faster and more nimble than butterflies. Why don't birds just eat them, particularly the big ones? The ongoing existence of butter-flies is an obvious flaw, an obvious wrinkle, in reality and the Theory.'

The VC, exhilarated that he has finally despatched his army, pounces with relish on his opponent's argument.

'Butterflies,' he says, 'are not to be underestimated. Like the Republic, they have multiple lines of defence. The first is their apparent size. They look much bigger than they are. The second is their use of optical tricks. Baffling colours. Dazzling patterns. Wing features that look like grabby limbs and boggly eyes. That sort of thing. And they have a last resort. They taste bad. I mean *really* bad. In their pupal stage they gorge themselves on milkweed, which birds can't stand. I assure you, boy, that butterflies are real, and that they coexist happily, for the most part, with birds.'

The delighted audience erupts in laughter and applause. And it gives the same response, too, when the VC knocks down effortlessly Will's proposition about the existence of daddy longlegs spiders – how, Will asks disastrously, can such little bodies drive such long limbs? Will Page's perfor-mance in the Midwinter Debate is rapidly turning into a steaming mess.

**30**

---

# A CURIOUS REVERSAL

As SOON AS the order is given, the Republican army of unreliable misfits crosses over into Inlandia. On the outer bank of the fast-flowing river they form up into divisions.

Tim Weston rushes to the front to see what's happening. Methodically the massing soldiers are lining up to drink from Inlandia's nourishing waters. One by one the divisions move forward to drink and then step aside to make way for the next rank of drinkers, who repeat the process.

Thanks to the magic of Inlandia, the ever-folding formations of soldiers are instantly upgraded, even ennobled. The Republican horde is slowly becoming a powerful and well-drilled machine. In their enhanced form the misfit soldiers will stand up well against Inlandia's defenders.

There isn't much time before the invaders make a move and begin their crossing. Tim's mind races. He is reluctant to join the battle, but he knows he must do something.

Earlier that day, every bell and alarm in Quincampoix had sounded. Inlandia's first line of defence – a hodgepodge flotilla of defiance – had immediately mobilised.

Fishing sloops, unaccustomed to actual battle, made their way from the sea into the river. The fishermen, armed only with nets and bill-hooks and makeshift flails, stood resolutely on the vessels' decks while the oldest among them led chants and cries that were as inspiring as they were baffling.

'For the Queen and Mkdos!'

'By de Rougemont's moustache!'

'For Bruno!'

Those inspiring cries are still ringing out when Tim finds the Spartans. They are gathered in strength on the fields to the west of the river. Some of them wear gilded armour. Some of them balance on rugged stilts, just like the ones de Rougemont used. And all of them are spoiling for a fight.

Tim pushes his way through the Spartan ranks in search of their leader. He soon finds Lord Krull, who is standing awkwardly, his arms out sideways as a squire fits his best armour.

'I know how to fight,' Tim says breathlessly. 'I even enjoy fighting sometimes. But I don't want to fight in this war…'

'I have no time for your Outlandish prattle,' Krull says. 'If you're not here to fight, get off the battlefield.'

Looking across Inlandia, Tim points to the tall aqueducts.

'I have a plan,' he says. 'All I need is five of your strongest soldiers. And three of your best plumbers.'

∞

Rani has a plan, too. With the archers of Mkdos she makes her way to the west bank. The river is wide, probably too wide, but Rani gives orders for bales of seasoned bunyip gut to be brought forward, so the archers can fortify their bows.

'Our weapons must be as strong as our convictions,' she tells her loyal archers. 'Today we must bend but not break. If the enemy won't come to us, then we must deliver our arrows to them.'

Soon those words have a desperate urgency. On the river's eastern bank, the Republican army has reached its full strength. The enemy vanguard wades into the shallows and begins to advance.

∞

Two storeys above the cottages of Quincampoix, Tim is putting his plan into action. Or at least he's trying to. His straining fingers grip the vertiginous stonework of a granite pillar that supports a central section of aqueduct. At the top of the pillar is a wheel-house and sluice valve that controls the flow of water from the banks of the river to the irrigated expanses of Inlandia.

This is the third such ascent he has made in the past hour. Elsewhere in Inlandia, two other teams are also working on the aqueducts, to Tim's precise directions.

Traditional aqueducts rely on gravity to move water. Since most of Inlandia's villages are on rising ground above the river, the Mkdoan aqueducts are different. In fact they're unique. Inlandia's engineers have crafted an ingenious wheel-valve-pump system that relies on a type of hydro-perpetual motion to carry water upwards through the sluice-ways.

Tim is more than competent as an amateur plumber. At Ashburnham he'd been called upon to solve all manner of hydrological emergencies. Now, in Inlandia, he knows the aqueduct system and he knows what he must do: stop the perpetual wheels from turning, while keeping the sluice-gates closed till all the valves are reversed. This work can only be done manually and with brute force – the way he and Will used to catch yabbies.

Tim ties a rope around his waist before wading chest-deep into the corralled water. The current pushes at him, threatening to drag him through the giant wooden wheel as it turns. To the side of the wheel, one of Lord Krull's best

Spartans braces himself against the water's force. Tim takes a deep breath and dives into the waterway.

At the bottom of the channel he grabs hold of a blade in the wheel. The flowing water twists him roughly. Instead of bringing the momentum to a halt, the blade wrenches from his grasp and jars his shoulder.

Without resurfacing, Tim reaches again for a sweeping blade. This time, planting his feet hard against the aqueduct's smooth granite floor, he halts the blade's progress. Straightening his back, he strains and stretches to his full height, breaking the surface just as a Mkdoan plumber jams a length of ironwood into the valve. With split-second timing, Tim drops the heavy bronze sluice-gate into place.

The water continues to flow away from his feet but the level is rapidly receding. As it drops below the height of his knees, Tim is reminded of the sensation he felt, standing on the surf beach near Port Phillip, when the waves washed back into the ocean, caressing him each time with a gentle undertow.

*It's working*, he thinks to himself. *It's working.*

Tim flashes a broad, 'mission accomplished' grin at his companions, then glances at the river to the east.

'Now we can have some fun.'

∞

Led by Rani's troop, a line of archers are now dotted along the western bank of the river. As the archers draw their bows, the taut strings cause the reinforced timbers to creak and groan.

'Release!'

At that command, a thousand arrows shriek across the river. The sound inspires the defenders and troubles the invaders. Until, that is, the arrows fall short. At least twenty yards short.

Cheering and emboldened, the Republican soldiers pick up their pace. More and more of them enter the water.

'We need more distance!' shouts Rani.

Grabbing two more lengths of cord, she swiftly drops and ties her feet to her bow. Then she rocks backward and, with both hands and all her strength, draws the bow-string and straightens her legs against the shaft, pushing the bow to the edge of its cooperation, and then beyond.

Like a comet, the loosed arrow drags a crackling shower of sparks. Alone in the air, Rani's missile silences the battlefield. All eyes watch as it arcs over the Mkdoan flotilla, over the Outlanders wading into the river, and over the far bank where it lands with a guttural thud in the shoulder of an Outlander titan who, by virtue of the Inlandian magic, towers above her former self and many of her comrades.

Rani's archers follow her example and soon the entire force of archers is reclining to draw their bows, feet first. The next volley makes the distance, finding targets across the battlefield. A great cry goes up from the Mkdoan side.

But the cry is premature. For every invader who stumbles in the face of the sparkling and whistling arrows, two more step forward. Energised rather than perturbed, the quickening invaders wade in vast numbers into the shallowest stretches of the rushing river.

∞

At Tim's command, the Spartans light a greenwood fire that sends a plume of white smoke skyward. It also sends a message. Soon, radiating out from Tim's position, pillar after pillar of white smoke reaches into the cloudless sky, forming an acrid chain of pillars all across Inlandia. These signals are met in turn with a sound: a faint shushing that quickly grows louder and more insistent. The plumbers have begun to reverse the flow.

Tim looks up to scan the aqueduct network. He watches in awe as the separate threads of diverted water move as one towards the eastern part of the system. The section in which Tim is waiting. As the threads begin to combine, the stone pillars begin to shake under the weight. Tim's awe turns to fear as sections of the stonework begin to crumble.

Along every causeway the crests of waves begin to crash past wheelhouses – hurtling toward the wheelhouse in which Tim is standing right now. He hears a dull boom as the nearest junction erupts in a roiling tumult of water. The flow rushes through the open valve and reduces the paddle-wheel to splinters.

'Get down!' Tim shouts to his team.

One of the Spartans climbs over the edge and begins his descent. Another takes a short-cut, dropping more than two storeys to terra firma. Tim makes a calculation and is about to trust his body to the same fall when he notices the plumber is still working on the sluice-gate. If the copper-lined gate stays shut, the pressure will wreck this whole section of aqueduct, and the diverted mass of water will spill uselessly to the ground.

Leaping from the waterway's edge to the small landing behind the gate, Tim gestures for the plumber to escape. Then, taking hold of the staff, he levers the sluice, but he isn't fast enough. The gate begins to bulge.

Tim strains and curses.

'Come on, you piece of...'

The barrier shunts open a third of the way before the shaft snaps, throwing Tim off balance. Wheeling his arms, he rocks back on his heels just as the wave swamps the wheel-house, obliterating the structure and taking Tim with it.

As the white water rushes over him and towards the river, he gasps for breath before disappearing with the snapped gate beneath the angry flow.

# 31

# A COLOSSUS

THOUSANDS OF MILES to the east, the Midwinter Debate rages on.

Let down by the animal kingdom, Will shifts speedily towards more mechanical – and hopefully more convincing – Inlandian truths.

'Record players,' he says, searching his mind for words the Teacher gave him. 'How can a single, uni-dimensional needle capture and transmit multiple tracks of music, multiple types of instrument, in multiple tones and pitches and volumes – all at the same time?'

'You're an odd boy and these are odd questions. Debating with you is like jousting with jelly. Do you seriously believe record players are instruments of magic or of devils? Do I really need to explain Edison's invention to you?'

Will changes the subject again, this time to skyscrapers.

'How can they stay up? Mountains are fatter at the bottom than the top. So, too, is bamboo. Vertical buildings face a basic problem. Every lower floor must hold up one after another of the higher ones. This all adds up to an exponential problem of weight. That's why, in Inlandia, all buildings are single or at most double storey, or pyramid-shaped.'

The VC's response is confident and immediate.

'Our scientists, architects and engineers have a full understanding of the physics of our towering buildings. This exponential weight objection has been voiced before. I've heard it myself. It's a popular fallacy, a furphy. The same claim could be made about slices of radio antennae, for example, or about tree branches, or blades of grass, not all of which are pyramids. In every skyscraper, the weight-bearing columns are built from materials that *gain* strength from compression. They're more than strong enough to hold the weight of higher floors, even in cyclones and earthquakes. What Will calls a fundamental problem is not a problem at all.'

Now toying with his opponent, the VC deploys his trademark intellectual flamboyance – and his trademark intellectual vanity.

'Young Will, you would've been on stronger ground if you'd asked about aeroplanes. We used to think differences in air pressure, above and below the wings, were what kept planes in the air. Now, though, we are certain it is something else. But we're not sure precisely what that something is. Aeroplanes are the subject of current research at Sandstone. Again, though, just like with record players, we are certain they do in fact work. I can assure you, Will, that planes do indeed fly!'

The VC adds a cruel and patronising flourish.

'I had such high hopes for you, but this debate is turning out to be yet another disastrous appearance on stage for a member of the Page family.'

∞

In Mkdos, whole stretches of the river are now masses of wading Republican soldiers. The fishermen hold fast in the mid-flow to parry with the invaders and disrupt their advance. Mkdoan arrows continue to whistle overhead, finding targets across the river and in the sloop-free sections of the water.

The fishermen have spent much of their lives on the sea and in the river. They know every ebb and every flow of the waters. Or perhaps not every flow.

As the fishermen look to the north, they see a rushing wall. A broiling mass of white foam. Everyone else sees it, too, including Rani.

Urgently she leads her troop further up the bank. The fishermen abandon their sloops, leaping overboard and diving below the surface to find refuge from the impending deluge. Much of the Republican army is stranded in the path of the wave. Helplessly the soldiers wade and tread water before the onslaught.

As the giant wave approaches, Rani sees a small shape at its centre. She can just make it out. Astride a copper board that shimmers in the afternoon sun, Tim Weston is riding the Mkdoan Bombora.

As the mass of water pushes through, it scatters soldiers and leaves chaos in its wake. The impact is felt on both sides but most heavily by the invaders. In the battle so far, this is their biggest setback. But they are many and they are resourceful. Soon they will regroup and redouble their efforts.

The main benefit of Tim's intervention is time. He has given the residents of Quincampoix and nearby villages precious minutes in which to flee north and west.

As the residents make their escape, the Mkdoan defenders pull back from the western bank to higher ground. They will make their stand at Quincampoix.

Tim, meanwhile, rides the wave all the way to the sea.

∞

Though formidable – and, increasingly, battle-hardened – the invading Outlander army is just one prong in a double attack on Inlandia. The much more dangerous assault, one that the Republic's leaders orchestrated and yet do not fully comprehend, strikes at the very foundations of Inlandia.

As Will falls further and further behind in the debate, the existence of Mkdos becomes more doubtful. A different kind of wave – one of Consistency, banality and annihilation – begins to spread across Inlandia. The wave is more powerful than the mishmash invasion force could ever be. And it's more devastating than Tim's watery one. It cuts deeply into the Mkdoan bedrock.

Assaulted by the advancing Consistency, Inlandia begins to shrink. Outlying villages disappear like corrected errors of logic. Penhadigon. Montpellier. Elizabethtowne. Gravesend. All these settlements are lost, replaced by stillness and void. And there is shrinkage, too, on the battlefield.

In the Great Hall of Sandstone University, two competing realities are duking it out. Like the pendulum of an enormous quantum clock, the debaters' fortunes cause reality to toggle between two states. The result is felt a thousand miles away, in the final phase of the strangest battle ever to be waged.

At the start of the battle, the invaders had taken on their enlarged Inlandian forms. But now, as the two sides finally meet each other in battle, the reality of Mkdos flickers, and the size and ferocity of the warriors fluctuates, too, according to the balance of the distant debate. Moment by moment, contests among titans become contests among minnows. Titanic arms become stick arms, then momentarily titanic, then momentarily sticks.

As the debate progresses, though, it turns more and more in the VC's favour. Thereafter, the fluctuations are mostly in one direction. On both sides of the oxymoronic battle, the soldiers shrink more than they grow. The Titan–minnows are mostly minnows.

Lord Krull, the war-hungry leader of the Spartans, demonstrates the fluctuations spectacularly. With every setback that Will suffers on stage, Krull becomes shorter, smaller, less fearsome. After the VC demolishes Will's technological arguments, Lord Krull shrinks to such an extent that, now, he is nothing more than old Mr Noakes, porter for hire.

∞

In the supercharged atmosphere of the Midwinter Debate, gloomy thoughts assail Will's mind. Grig's worst tidings have come true. Will has let Inlandia down. He has failed his parents and Jenny and Rani. All hope for him and his loved ones is lost.

It was only adrenaline that allowed him to overcome his fears and climb on stage at the start of the debate. Now, the adrenaline rush fading, those fears race back. His inner voice screams at him.

*Flee! Flee!*

In a panic he scans the audience – an unsympathetic sea of scornful faces. One face, though, has a different expression, one of thoughtful concern. The face belongs to the VC's beautiful, unreachable daughter, Laura Macdonald, sitting in the front row. Will can't help but notice the girl who was his childhood obsession. He notices, too, the gourd-shaped object that she cradles in her lap.

It's about the size of a softball but shaped like a rounded hourglass, with two bulbous ends and a pinched middle. Delicate little cracks cover the smooth glossy surface.

The object's map-like markings loosely resemble the outlines of planet Earth's continents. But the object is certainly not a sphere. Seeing it reminds Will of the rumours he heard. Second-hand Inlandian rumours, relayed by the Teacher, about the history and shape of the world.

Desperate, he blurts out one last proposition.

'The world,' he says, 'was not always round.'

The audience erupts in anger and boos of derision. The boy has voiced an offensive heresy, a bald-faced contradiction of Mandelbrot's Theory. Will's assertion is a red rag especially to the VC and the Republic. It is one, though, that those powers are well equipped to rebut.

And yet the VC's face tells a different story. As he considers Will's proposition, Macdonald remembers all the imperfections he glossed over as Keeper of the Consistency Engine. All the adjustments he made and the tricks he used to reconcile the Engine and to maintain Consistency upon our imperfect, inexact sphere of a planet.

He remembers, too, a feeling that he often had when he was a junior chemical engineer working in his lab. A feeling that reality was malleable, and that, in the course of his research, he was *creating* rather than discovering the properties of existence; that he was *writing* the story of reality, not just *reading* it.

Thanks to these turbulent thoughts, an unprecedented thing happens. Oliver Macdonald, the illustrious Vice Chancellor of Sandstone University, scion of the Republic, protector of the Theory, is filled with doubt.

And then he, too, scans the audience and he, too, notices the object on his daughter's lap. Immediately he sees its meaning and significance. Immediately he remembers the stories his grandmother told him. Secret stories about a different kind of world and a different way of living. Stories he always dismissed.

The pinched globe is the one valuable thing he inherited from his parents and grandparents. He'd been fascinated by it since childhood, and had taught himself to interpret it as a physical metaphor, perhaps for how the present is a mere pinch between the infinite past and the infinite possibilities of the future. That interpretation, he now sees, is very likely wrong. Had his grandmother confided in him a much more concrete secret?

All confidence leaves the VC's face as he considers the pocket globe that isn't a globe at all but an hourglass map of the world. These are forbidden ideas, in direct contradiction to the Theory. But hasn't he already entertained heretical thoughts? Hasn't he already acknowledged the possible presence of a significant anomaly in reality, by sending first Loopy and then the Republic's freakish army to the interior?

Suddenly unsteady on his feet, the VC asks for a chair and a glass of water. The audience notices in shock this display of weakness, occurring as it has in a debate between the VC and a disowned and trespassing child. People begin to shout. Security guards make a move to mount the stage and seize the VC's opponent. And then the whole auditorium shakes, as though a tremor has barrelled through reality.

A convulsive, uncontrollable gasp bursts into the air. Everybody freezes. Then they hear a terrifying sound. The sound of gigantic metal footsteps, followed by a crashing noise as the doors of the hall smash open.

Standing twenty feet tall in the wrecked doorway is an unmistakable figure. A great golden man. A mechanical colossus.

In a deafening metallic voice, the Consistency Engine speaks four tectonic words.

'THE. BOY. IS. RIGHT.'

# 32

## THE ENGINE'S KEEPER

NO ONE HAS EVER SEEN the Consistency Engine walk. And they've certainly never heard it talk. At the conclusion of the debate, Will leads the Engine back to its home in the Chamber of Logic. He is its Keeper now.

The very moment that the Engine spoke in the debate, the war was won and Inlandia returned to its original extent. And then it kept growing. Faster than the news could spread, waves of existence propagated outward from Inlandia and transformed the whole world into the Mkdoan reality.

The invading soldiers, now permanently fixed in their enhanced Inlandian shape, laid down their arms. And, as the transforming wave advanced, other wonderful things happened.

The continent of Australia was suddenly greener, more colourful, and more exotic. Outside Inlandia, bunyips and minyips had only ever been glimpsed in remote billabongs and in the upper reaches of the Murrumbidgee River. Now, though, they appear in many places in plain sight. More and more households will soon adopt minyips as pets.

On the continent's south coast, more mahogany ships will soon be uncovered, along with implements that date from the time of the Bellarine Keys. Around the world, everyone will be enlarged and enlivened by the Mkdoan fountain of youth.

But many of the wave's effects are terrible. Thanks to Will's victory in the debate, the Inlandians have won the argument about tall buildings. Every building on Earth that is not pyramid-shaped, and is taller than two storeys, collapses.

Most people have enough warning and can escape in time. But many are warned too late or not at all. Many people are killed, and many more are injured.

There are other casualties, too. All the world's butterflies disappear, along with pelicans and daddy longlegs. And the moon.

Everything that depends on electricity and electronics stops working. The transport system. Machines in hospitals. All digital devices.

In a surprisingly short time, the world adjusts to these new conditions. Gas and candles are used for light. Steam engines and hot air balloons for mass transit. Letters and flags for communication. Difference-engines and slide-rules for computing. Apart from gas-power and candlepower, cities soon come to rely on horsepower – and bunyip-power.

Almost everyone is at a loss as to why the buildings fell, and why electricity and appliances no longer work. Maybe gravity changed, some scientists conjecture. Or maybe a surge of terrible earthquakes somehow damaged the earth's magnetic field. But Will and John Page know the truth.

A curious feature of the new reality is that people quickly forget what life was like before the transformation. Relying on simple, pre-modern technologies becomes the natural thing to do, as does building pyramidally or to a low-rise height. Almost imperceptibly, the strange becomes normal.

Apart from the widespread destruction and dislocation, victory in the debate causes an international power vacuum.

The Republic and its allies immediately lose their authority. After the debate, the euphoric Mkdorii can leave Inlandia freely and travel to the coast and beyond. In time, the freed Inlandians fill the vacuum. With an institution called the New Regime, the Inlandian monarchy begins to rule the world.

∞

In the midst of the Mkdoan euphoria, John Page is freed from the great pyramid's dungeon. With the inland reality now pre-eminent, what harm can he do? As two small parts of the Inlandian exodus, he and Rani Sharma make plans to leave for the coast. Tim Weston decides to stay in the interior. There, he thinks, he might teach, perhaps write some poetry, and search out the surfable breaks of the inland sea.

As soon as John and Rani cross the old frontier between Inlandia and the Outland, they come upon Alan Smith. Will and Rani were right all along. Their shadow was the assassin, not the janitor.

John knows much about the Actuaries: what they are taught, and of what they are capable. As soon as Smith stands before him, he knows why the assassin is here.

'We've much in common,' John says. 'We both encounter the world precisely as it is, not just as we wish it to be.'

Smith sees the truth in this. Thanks to his arduous training, he has acquired a peculiarly scientific way of seeing the world. Observant, methodical, detached. Sometimes, he even glimpses the provisional, flickering nature of reality. And in his calmest, most meditative moments, he can feel the infinitely subtle backwash of collapsing quantum waves.

'You don't need to kill me now,' John says. 'Inlandia has won. The Republic is finished.'

In one smooth movement, the assassin unsheathes his

stiletto blade and drives it neatly, purposefully into John Page's beating heart.

The former professor drops to the ground.

'How could you!' Rani screams at the assassin. 'How could you!'

Horrified, she draws her bow and aims an arrow at John Page's killer, who stands before her, arms wide. She has shot her arrows at straw-filled targets. And she has shot at great distances across the battlefield. But till now she has never looked into a target's eyes, especially none so cold and dispassionate as those before her.

Alan Smith notices her hesitation, understands what it means. Wordlessly he turns away, then walks purposefully northwards. When the assassin disappears from view, Rani does her best to bury John's body. After some improvised words of prayer, she sets out alone, eastward, back along the route she followed with Will.

Longing to reunite with Rani, Will retraces that same route in the opposite direction. When, a few weeks later, the pair meet on the track, they weep for John, and for Jenny, and for all the others they've lost.

Though he doesn't say so to Rani, Will fears his father has joined the floating souls in the Underworld, where he will for ever be prey to monsters, and to an immense, seductive, dreadful nothingness.

∞

When Will and Rani arrive in Port Phillip, they reunite with Queen Mary, who inducts them formally into the new royal court and the royal household that rules the world.

The Queen has already made plans for a coastal pyramid-palace, to be constructed upon the ruins of Port Phillip's collapsed central business district. The new pyramid, to be built using gold from Lasseter's Reef, will be even larger and more spectacular than the one at Quincampoix.

In the meantime, she occupies the Vice Chancellor's office at Sandstone University, whose old stone buildings with their strong foundations have largely escaped the destruction. Everyone in the kingdom sees the Queen's occupation of the VC's office as symbolic of absolute victory – in the history war as well as the actual war.

From that office, the Queen issues a series of proclamations. By royal decree, she announces that the scientific revolution was a failure, a disastrous wrong turn. It, along with the doctrine of Consistency and any limits on her royal authority, are consigned to the technicoloured wheelie-bin of history.

The Queen also publishes an official list of martyrs and victims – the people who were persecuted for contradicting the Theory of Everything or questioning the sanctioned History of the World. Her own name is prominent on the list.

Another proclamation announces that wartime traitors and criminals will be put on trial. A chief prosecutor will be appointed, along with a team of investigators. The Queen herself will sit in judgement, with Lord Krull by her side as chief advisor.

Will and Rani move into adjoining quarters in one of the old colleges on the leafy northern edge of the Sandstone campus. They resume their routine of taking evening walks, and become more and more comfortable in each other's company. As members of the royal entourage, they have many official duties – opening new schools, launching new airships, reviewing new laws – and they perform many of these duties together.

Will also has official duties as Keeper of the Engine. He spends most mornings in the Chamber of Logic, studying the great machine and getting to know its personality and its quirks. Having found its voice, the Engine confides in Will, marvelling at the wonders of the present day and the mysteries of the ancient past.

The finely tuned machine knows a great deal about the goings on at Sandstone and beyond. By detecting subtle vibrations – and by intercepting digital messages – it has eavesdropped on all the Great Hall events and much else besides. Evidently the Engine has long been a diligent observer and a sensitive spy. Its neat and enormous catalogue of knowledge contains more than a few secrets about the world and its human masters.

Perhaps as a result of its fractal construction, the Engine seems to be primed to find fractal patterns in space and time. It notices how the shapes of veins in bodies and plants are repeated at a geographical scale in river deltas and lightning, and at a celestial one in galactic filaments and clusters. And it notices recurring patterns in art, culture, politics and all other fields of human endeavour. Humans themselves, the Engine thinks, are utterly intriguing. So small and vulnerable, and yet so often blind to their frailty.

Will interrogates the Engine about its surprise appearance at the Midwinter Debate. What did it mean, exactly, when the Engine said Will was right? The interrogation doesn't get far. The Engine will only say that the structure of the world has long been debated, and was once much simpler.

On his evening walks with Rani, Will shares what he learns each day from the Engine. How it works and how it thinks. In Inlandia, Will had felt left out of his mother's rise to fame. Now, in Port Philip, he's in the thick of it. For him, this period of managing the Engine and – with his mother and Rani – managing the world, is a golden time.

And then the war-crime trials begin.

# 33

# THE TRIALS

ALAN SMITH's trial is first.

Will arrives early at the Great Hall, the very place where he won the Midwinter Debate. Casually he checks the back of the hall, but the damage caused by the Engine has long since been repaired, the new timbers painted over. He takes his seat.

Soon the Queen arrives, too, along with Lord Krull and a contingent of officials and gawkers and hangers-on. The prosecutor addresses the now-packed hall-cum-courtroom.

'Smith was a member of a wicked sect of assassins who called themselves the Actuaries. The New Regime has disbanded the group, rounded up its members, shut down their monasteries.'

'This defendant is of great interest to me,' the Queen says, before addressing Smith directly. 'I knew your brother. What can you tell me of his role in my expedition to the interior?'

'His orders were to remain with your party till it reached the point of no return. Then he was supposed to provoke maximum mayhem, with lethal force if necessary. There were many things he could've done. Pick a fight, make it seem as though someone else started it. Destroy equipment. Sow ill-feeling and despair. Probably he did all these things. He took no food or water of his own. He tied his fate to the party. It was a suicide mission.'

'A homicide mission, don't you mean,' the Queen says angrily. 'Your brother killed Zouche. And if it weren't for Inlandia, his sabotage would've killed us all.'

The prosecutor reads the charges for a serious crime committed after the war was won: the murder of John Page, the Queen's husband and Inlandia's Prince Consort.

Smith speaks briefly in his defence. He had searched for John, before following Will inland.

'Without the crack of a twig or the rustle of a grass-blade, I followed the young master from Redcliffe. After Murnania, where the young lady joined him, I followed them both. When the pair later entered the inland place, I saw them fade away. They were passing through a frontier that was closed to me. So I waited. Much later, I saw the young master escape, along with a misshapen boy. They'd used a secret route. But, when the world changed, John Page simply walked out.'

'And you killed him,' the Queen says sharply.

For Smith, the murder was especially important. It was a way to anchor himself in reality. A way to affirm his identity. A matter of reassurance. An act of fulfilment.

'Yes I did. I killed him because I'm a killer. That's what I do. I could kill all of you now, if I so wished. Swiftly. Neatly. But that's not my mission. I only kill when instructed to do so, and I only take orders from the true government. That is, from the Republic. You, Mary Page, are a usurper. A trouble-maker. A Yippy vandal. It was *your* hubris that doomed your expedition and caused my brother's death. Do what you will with me, but I'll have no more truck with this kangaroo court.'

The furious Queen immediately pronounces Smith guilty of capital murder. She orders that he be locked in irons and sent away. Except by the soldiers and warders who take him to an unknown location, he will never be seen or heard of again in this world.

191

# A COSMOLOGICAL HERESY

ACCORDING to the Queen's war-crimes proclamation, the next defendant will be Oliver Macdonald, formerly Vice Chancellor of Sandstone University. His trial is due in two days' time. In advance of the trial, Laura calls on Will in his chambers. And she brings the globe.

Laura had filched the object from an antique chest in her attic. Buried under moth-eaten blankets and silverfished prints. The chest is where her father used to hide things. His most secret and valuable things, some of them certainly not suitable for the most senior academic in the Republic. But that hardly matters now.

'I like to keep it with me,' Laura says. 'It's a comfort. I take it all kinds of places. The shops, museums, libraries. I've been researching it. How it was made, where it came from. Its connection to my grandparents, and to their parents and their parents' parents. Turns out my ancestors were linked to some sort of cult. They knew your ancestors, too.'

'We might even be cousins,' Will says jokingly, awkwardly.

Laura pulls the velvet-lined morocco case from her canvas bag and opens it. The globe seems to have grown since Will last saw it. Perhaps, he thinks, the growth is one more side-effect of the Inlandian takeover.

The markings are now easier to read, as are the key and insignia that sit slap bang in the centre of a massively enlarged Antarctica.

Will studies the map. The names and shapes of its continents and islands. There are no East or West Indies. Just 'The Indies'. Most of the Sahara is under water, and the northern part of what would otherwise be Africa is labelled 'Atlantis'. In North America, California is an island. And Canada, like Antarctica, is massively stretched. So too, in Eurasia, the territories of Russia and Outer Mongolia are vastly expanded as part of the enormous northern continents.

Inverse to the growth in those landmasses is the shrinkage of southern India, the Indian Ocean, the mid-Atlantic and especially the Pacific.

Laura shares what she has learnt.

'The insignia is the infinity symbol,' she says, 'surrounded by the words *Novum Organum*. That's Latin. It means "New instrument". As in scientific instrument, not musical. On the way to the interior there's a town called Murnania. You probably travelled through there. I went there, too. It's full of peculiar people, little affected by the new reality. Some of them remain loyal to the Republic, others to even earlier masters. The town has a strange library. It was once very grand and much used. By the time of my visit it had fallen into disarray. I had to scramble over fallen bookshelves and wade through pulpy puddles. An enormous termite-mound, the colour of red brick, stood in the centre of the main reading room – so large I could climb inside and browse the strange, natural labyrinth. In one of its chambers, I found what remained of the library's catalogue. According to that record, the library's holdings included rare manuscripts, such as the diaries of William Buckley and Louis de Rouge-mont. Early printed books, too, beautifully bound in cream leather. But the catalogue dated from an era that was long gone. Now, most of the books were falling apart. Food for the termites as well as cockroaches and other creatures. A disgrace, really.

'The townsfolk knew little of why or by whom the library was built. They were happy, nonetheless, for me to take books away. I borrowed one that was written in the style of a novel but may in fact be a true, alternative history of the world. The volume is a little mystery. I don't know who wrote it. When I came across it, the cover and first pages were missing. But the middle chapters spoke of a cosmological heresy in strange terms like the Northern and Southern Bulges and the Great Pinch. There was a section on Skiing the Pinch – apparently not possible – and one on using telescopes to gaze across the Great Valley and look down on other lands – apparently entirely possible. The book spoke of the Indies as a band of islands extending all the way round the Pinch. Permanent mists and temporary waterfalls stretched across the pit of the Great Valley, fortifying the Indies with rain and runoff. Nourished in this way, the author wrote, the Indies became the garden of the world, its greatest source of natural wealth.'

Will marvels in awe at this profusion of wonders. The beauty and strangeness of the hourglass globe. Earth's garden, not on the nipple of a pear but in the pit of a connecting Pinch. And North and South as two thinly attached spheres, almost two separate worlds, like the left and right hemispheres of a planetary brain.

He marvels, too, at how much his life has changed since an accident of alphabetical ordering put him behind Laura at Ashburnham High. A little less than a year ago, the idea of being alone with her and her brown, braided hair would've been an unthinkable delight. Now, up close and face to face, he notices for the first time the topaz highlights in her eyes.

'Other parts of the book,' Laura says, 'dealt with the weird geology and ocean currents around the Pinch. The book is full of riddles and absurdities, such as how Telluric currents can be used to sculpt our planet, and how the Earth moves in cyclical, epicyclical, eccentric and equantic orbits. The final chapters expressed the author's fears about returning to what she called the world's natural shape. If, she conjectured, the Bulges were connected only by the narrow shaft of the Pinch, could a meteor or an earthquake break them apart? Might they then crash into each other in a catastrophic collision? Or would they instead enter a harmless orbit, circling each other in a never-ending dance?'

'I heard similar things,' Will says, 'in Inlandia, about the East and West Indies being joined, and about the constriction of the globe. And about the cult.'

'Despite its deplorable condition,' Laura says, 'the Murnanian book is not so very old. Members of the cult might still be active. With the Inlandian takeover, you've shown that the world can be changed. Cultists, possibly through allies in the New Regime, might push for this shape to be adopted. And that would be a disaster. The atom bomb would be nothing in comparison. You've got to talk to the Engine, convince it to never change. Or to change back.'

'To the Republic? You must be kidding.'

'The Republic wasn't so bad. Not so hazardous or offensive as historians and intellectuals now say. And its people, for the most part, were not so wicked. I know for certain that my father is a good man, if a little strict. And pompous.'

'I knew that's why you'd come. To speak for your father. He was a terrible leader, in a terrible government. Do you not remember the assassins? And the war against Inlandia? The daily fears and intrigues? All the nonsense about Consistency? All the rotten rules about who could marry whom, and about what we were allowed to think? You've forgotten what the world was really like. How people actually lived under the arrogant, treacherous, lethal Republic.'

'The Actuaries killed maybe three or four people a year,' Laura says quietly. 'Every murder was in the service of the public good. In the war, the invaders fought soldiers, not civilians. And they lost. After the Inlandian victory, falling buildings and powerless hospitals killed thousands, maybe hundreds of thousands. The old regime was subject to checks and balances. Where are the checks and balances now? Are we to believe Lord Krull will keep the New Regime on track?'

## THE COIN TOSS

THE FOLLOWING DAY, Will again arrives early at the Great Hall. He is determined not to miss the trial in which Queen Mary will face off against the man who, at a very different forum, defeated her so convincingly. Now, as Will watches her take her seat at the bench of the makeshift courtroom, she is in every respect the victor.

Laura is another early arrival. Dressed in what looks like mourning clothes – black dress, black stockings, black shawl – she sits with her mother, her brother Todd, and the few academics who prospered under the Republic and yet have the courage to now be seen in public with a Macdonald. From across the hall, Todd notices Will – and his eyes send bitter daggers in the direction of his former classmate.

At the appointed time, guards escort the ex-VC into the Hall. The downcast, defrocked high-priest of Consistency. Stripped of all his honours and titles, Macdonald appears in humble clothes and, indeed, without any of the trappings of his former office. He appears, that is, as plain Mr Macdonald – a broken man with nothing to say in his defence. His whole world, quite literally, has collapsed.

In a grave, low-pitched voice the prosecutor reads a long

list of charges, the worst of which are heresy, fraud, treason, murder, abuse of office, and making war on the kingdom.

As Laura weeps in the audience, a resigned Oliver Macdonald acknowledges the charges but makes no effort to contest them. Instead he just nods feebly before muttering something that is barely audible.

'History must always be written by the victorious.'

In short order he is led away, guilty as charged. The Queen feels an immense disappointment at not being able to debate him a second time.

Macdonald's brief and anti-climactic appearance frees up the court's schedule, so the court moves immediately to the trial of Tim Weston.

Tim Weston? Will can't believe it. As the Queen's son, Will has a senior role in the royal household. And yet he had no idea that his old friend was in Port Phillip, and in custody. He had no warning that Tim would face trial in this way.

He looks on in shock as the trial begins. Tim is led in. The prosecutor accuses him of high treason.

'Your Majesty. The Republic sent the defendant to spy on Inlandia. His presence there was the trigger that confirmed for the Vice Chancellor that our interior civilisation existed and, indeed, thrived. We know this from our interrogation of Mr Macdonald. In a direct and culpable sense, the defendant betrayed the kingdom and caused the invasion.'

'You could just as well argue,' Tim interjects, 'that I *saved* Inlandia, not just through my actions on the battlefield but by helping to sow doubt in Macdonald's mind about the Outland reality, and by helping Will to win the debate and then the war. The Republic may have sent me but they never trusted me. I was never an insider. "Unreliable." "Crazy." "The product of a disreputable marriage." "Just enough tainted blood to breach the wall." That's what they said and that's why they chose me. People said the same kinds of things in the Inland. "Tainted blood." I've been hearing that, and much worse, ever since I was a kid. But, growing up, I did my best at school, even though all the advantages, all the opportunities, were barred to me. I got the best job I could, and mostly did what I was told. In the war I did my best to delay the worst of the fighting. I tried to keep faith with both sides. I was sure, after all, that one of them would win. And the two sides weren't so different anyhow. There are good people on every side in every war, just as there is good and bad in every person. Knowing that is why I'm such a reluctant soldier, such an unsuitable spy. There are benefits, though, from being an outsider. You hear all sorts of things. You notice how cruel and foolish people can be. And what lies they tell. Peaceful, warlike. Primitive, sophisticated. Old, new. Open, closed. Known, unknown. I've heard every kind of claim about Inlandia. Mkdoan history contains as much nonsense and as many lies as the history of the Republic and the Theory of Everything. You're making it all up as you go along, just as the Outlanders were. You think you've won the argument about what the world should be like. But how can this Mkdoan world be real? How can it be primary if there's no moon?'

The whole courtroom gasps at this heresy, and the lunar memories it ushers back.

'We've lost the world's second source of light,' Tim says. 'The sun's complement. The surfer's friend. The inspiration for every poet since Homer. This new reality is no more valid than the old Republican one. In many ways, it's worse.'

With that the court erupts, only coming to order when the prosecutor gestures for silence. Then he addresses the Queen.

'I don't think we need to hear any more from this defendant. He is obviously guilty, your grace.'

The court erupts again, this time in assent and jubilation.

Will Page can't believe what is happening. He shouts over the clamour.

'Let me speak! Let me speak!'

All as one the people in the Great Hall turn their faces and their attention towards the prince. He clears his throat, choking back fear and anger.

'I've known Tim since I was seven years old,' Will says. 'He's eccentric, that's for sure. Often reckless. But he was always a good friend to me, even when others shunned my friendship. Even when . . .' Will falters as he recalls the grand reception. 'Even when I wasn't a good friend to him. I appeal to the court. Show mercy towards Tim Weston. And I appeal, too, for the Queen's mercy towards the former Vice Chancellor. For Oliver Macdonald.'

These words provoke shock and dismay in the court. A member of the royal household is speaking in favour of one of the most despised leaders of the old Republic.

The prosecutor again gestures for silence. Once the court has composed itself, the Queen speaks.

'You are a good and kind boy, Prince William. Everyone here knows that. And you've been through so much that you would have me grant mercy to all the kingdom's enemies. As a gesture of royal grace, I'll grant half your request. You've spoken in favour of two defendants. I'll send one of them to prison. The other will share the fate of the assassin, Alan Smith. A coin toss will decide.'

## DE-SPHERING

IN THE COURTROOM, Lord Krull had struggled to hide his rage. After the court adjourns, he and two Spartan guards visit Will in his quarters. The guards stand just inside the door. Krull paces the living room, occasionally picking up a book or a piece of paperwork and regarding it with blatant contempt.

'A brave move indeed. Defending the old VC like that. And your friend Tim, too. Weston was right, you know, about this being an unsatisfactory reality. We are still trapped in the Republic's Copernican world. I have high hopes for you as Keeper. Together, we have to move to the next phase of remaking the world. We need to revert to a more primary shape. We need to de-sphere.'

Will gives the chieftain a look of sudden awareness and doubt. Krull continues.

'Sir Francis Bacon published *Novum Organum* in 1620. The book was a scientific masterpiece, the pinnacle of his life's work. It marked a new era in scholarship. Bacon wrote that printing and gunpowder and the compass had changed the shape of the world. This was a message to his followers. A message that, before the seventeenth century, the world wasn't spherical. Over the centuries, the original shape of the world has been debated. Was Planet Earth a tight cylinder, such that Newfoundland and Kamchatka were the same place, and likewise New South Wales and Argentina, and Tasmania and Tierra del Fuego? Was it an oval, with deeper oceans at the poles? Was it a Klein Bottle, with an endless surface? Or a disc, held up by props, or by elephants on the back of a giant Wingilpin turtle? I know you've seen the true shape of the world. The original shape. The hourglass globe. According to one legend, the hourglass pinch and bulges were made when a great serpent constricted an elongated, tube-shaped world, one with vast icy wastes to the north and south. Personally I'm not a fan of that theory. I believe the hourglass shape came first. How do I know? Because that shape is revealed in *Novum Organum*. Bacon's printer produced a special edition of the treatise, one reserved for private circulation among Sir Francis's closest followers. The title page of that edition depicts the world as two spheres. And if you use a special decoder to read the mysterious text on that page, you find HOUR and GLASS. All the evidence is there if you know how to look for it.'

*Novum Organum.* The words on Laura's globe. They reverberate in Will's ears. Lord Krull is a secret cultist. A Baconian heretic.

'Copernicus committed terrible, reckless crimes,' Krull says. 'His sphering of the globe was a disaster for millions of people. The spice islands were split into East and West. The vast Southern Land – much larger than the continents of Australia and South America and Antarctica combined – was broken up, its coasts pushed back, many of its inhabitants killed. De-sphering would repair that land and make good a grave injustice. And imagine the new world! A restored Atlantis. The marvellous island of California. The Southern Land returned to its grandeur and its might. We must start reshaping the Earth right away. As victor in the debate and as

Keeper of the Engine, you're naturally the one to lead the de-sphering. You're naturally the one to reverse Copernicus's damage. You need to go to the Chamber of Logic right now and convince the Engine.'

Will knows what danger he is in. He knows the stakes. All his instincts scream caution.

'Why can't we wait?' he says, choosing his words carefully. 'Maybe we can think about it some more. Yes there would be marvels, but horrors, too. For the islands that would sink. And for the continents and oceans that would shrink.'

'You don't need to worry about any of that. We've taken precautions. The kingdom's armies are moving people out of the most vulnerable areas. We've set up camps. On the edge of the Sahara and in Central India and Central America.'

'I won't do it,' Will says quietly, hearing Laura's voice in his head and feeling her words on his lips. 'At least, not straight away. Not till I know for sure what the risks are, and how the world's peoples would benefit. I've been faced with decisions like this before and I already have much to regret. Falling skyscrapers and power failures killed thousands. De-sphering could kill millions.'

Krull stops hiding his anger.

'Enough of this stalling. I hereby relieve you of your duties as Keeper. You've brought disgrace to that venerable post. I'll appoint a new Keeper, one who can do the job that needs to be done. Guards, take Prince William to the dungeon.'

The Spartan guards confiscate Will's pocket cannon before leading him down ladders and stairs to the deepest, dampest tunnels underneath Sandstone University. There, work teams are putting the finishing touches on the temporary cells of a temporary dungeon – a hastily built makeshift that will serve the kingdom while a proper dungeon is constructed in the new pyramid-palace.

Coming to an empty cell, the guards throw Will inside.

His mind races. This whole thing must be part of a palace coup. Lord Krull and his fellow cultists must be taking over. Queen Mary is in danger, along with all the other Athenians. The entire kingdom, for that matter. And if the cultists get their way then God help the whole world.

# A CRUEL TRUTH

IN THE IMPROVISED dungeon beneath Sandstone, a few minutes pass. Then Will hears a nearby voice. Muffled. Familiar.

'I hope, Rabbit Page, that you're proud of your creation. I hope you're proud of this backward, moonless, poor excuse for a world.'

The voice belongs to Tim Weston. It's coming from the cell next door.

'Thanks to you,' Tim continues, 'we've swapped one obnoxious dictatorship for another. One set of obsessive, power-corrupted despots for another. These phoney Greeks might even be worse than the previous lot. They're really starting to get on my nerves.'

Will waits several moments before saying anything. In the meantime he absorbs and savours this unexpected meeting and all that it implies. To hear Tim's voice again, no matter how angry or cheesed off he is, fills Will with gratitude and relief. When eventually he speaks, he is calm, reflective, even happy.

'I feel,' he says, 'strangely at home here.'

He and Tim had long ago mastered the world below

Sandstone. Now they are back. And Will can see, too, the irony and the symmetry of his imprisonment.

'I was expelled from school the same day my father was fired from the physics department, do you remember? Now I'm here, in a dungeon, emulating him in yet another way. I never thought I'd follow in his footsteps so literally.'

'So,' Tim says, 'what happens now?'

'Lord Krull wants to use the Engine to reshape the world. We've got to stop him. We have to get a message to my mother, if she hasn't been got to already.'

∞

In the end, contacting Mary is much easier than Will and Tim expected. On the second day of Will's captivity, his cell door opens and she appears unbidden in his doorway.

'Are you here as a prisoner,' he says in shock and amazement, 'or a rescuer?'

'A rescuer of course. But first there's something I must ask of you. I need you to make peace with Lord Krull. He can be part of our household, part of our family. A King for your Queen. And a stepfather to you, I suppose, which would make Jenny in death your stepsister. What a powerful team we'd be! Together, we can peel back all the Republic's lies. Move to a truer, more ancient reality. The hourglass planet. The proof and pinnacle of all my theories, all my work.'

Will doesn't need to say anything in reply. Mary can read his face just as she could read his father's. Will's reaction is a bitter brew of disbelief, disillusionment and disappointment.

He puts no store in his mother's grandiose, triumphal talk. More than once, he has seen a so-called triumph turn out to be anything but. And in regard to the Queen's principal adviser, her favourite Spartan, Will could never accept him as any kind of father. And to invoke Jenny in this way, as a perverse kind of sweetener or bargaining chip. That is unforgivable, an insult to her memory. These are the thoughts that jostle in his mind.

Will glances at the abundant rings that adorn his mother's fingers. Up close, he now thinks, they look more crass than regal. And he notices something for the first time. One of the rings bears the same infinity insignia as the hourglass globe. And, inscribed in tiny, encircling letters, the same words.

*Novum Organum.*

And then, again for the first time, Will sees his mother for what she is. A bolter. A Baconian. A co-conspirator with Lord Krull. Probably also his lover.

Even before she was made Queen, Mary Page had long accepted most of the theories that, according to the Teacher, are central to the cultists' beliefs. She must've long been a member of the Baconian sect. The Spartan–Athenian conflict must be a blind, a diversion. Civil war was never a real danger in Inlandia. Knowingly or not, the Teacher misled Will. He's as unreliable as de Rougemont. Mary and Krull pulled the strings all along. The Athenian leaders are just as bad as the Spartans. Tim and Laura are right. With Mary and Krull in charge, the Mkdoan kingdom is just as bad as the Republic.

As Will's thoughts continue to jostle, Mary continues to read most of them on his face. She knows right away that, whatever happens, he will never submit.

'Members of our secret society,' she says coolly, 'were told of a prophecy. A new Adam, the prophecy said, would come forth and remake the world. I never thought it would be you. You were always so . . . orthodox. So unimpressive. But, after your debate, I began to think I might be wrong. Now, though, I know I was right. And if you look around you, you'll notice that I'm pretty well always right.'

Will remembers what de Rougemont had said of the Mkdos tribe.

*Little known, but cruel.*

'After you left dad and me,' Will says quietly, 'the gossips in Redcliffe accused you of abandoning us. They called you selfish. Said you cared more about your theories than your family. Dad and I always defended you.'

Mary reflects on this for a moment.

'If you can't cooperate,' she says finally, 'then stay out of the New Regime's affairs.'

Stepping from her son's cell, the High Queen of Inlandia – and the World – slams the door behind her.

A few moments later, Will hears four whispered words from the neighbouring cell.

'I never liked her.'

38

## A STRANGE BOND

Weeks pass.

Will and Tim maintain an intermittent, hushed dialogue through narrow cracks and gaps in the cinderblock partition that separates their cells.

Like two seasoned jailbirds, they share stories from their youth.

'Do you remember Jan's Cafe?' Will asks. 'The old milk-bar in Redcliffe where we played Space Invaders and table soccer? I always had to buy you chips.'

'Do you remember the anatomy class,' Tim replies, 'and the brain?'

As that memory and its vivid images leap into their minds, both inmates have the same thought. Could the meaty, fleshy thing on the cold steel table really be where all human experience is had and made? All the art, the poetry, the science, the love?

No. The fleshy brain is as much a fiction as the empty interior of Australia.

∞

For long stretches of time, both inmates are silent. Will's mind embraces the quiet. As he falls into a kind of trance, all the words he heard on his quest now return and swirl around him. He can see and feel their power. The words of his parents and the VC and the Engine. Those of Loopy, Rani, Grig and Laura. And the precious, fleeting words of Jenny. All these words – and all the stories they made – swim in his mind and seem even to shape the space around him. He can read floating, illuminated words in the air and on the walls of his cell. Though entirely imaginary, just a projection of his unstimulated mind, they seem more tangible than the stone and steel and concrete of his prison.

∞

'It can't have happened yet,' Will whispers to Loopy, breaking the silence. 'The de-sphering. I'm sure we'd feel it. Krull and my mother mustn't be able to find the right Keeper. Or the Keeper mustn't be able to convince the Engine.'

Soon a visitor arrives at the makeshift dungeon.

Wearing a sari with gold embellishments, Rani Sharma looks stunningly beautiful. The pair of ogling guards – Tim has christened them Rosencrantz and Guildenstern – refuse to let her inside Will's cell. So instead she grasps his fingers eagerly through the barred hole in his door.

'Pulled a lot of strings to get here,' she says breathlessly. 'Strings with those in the kingdom who still regard me technically as a member of the royal household. And strings among those, still loyal to the old Republic, who see me as sympathetic to their cause, on account of my connection to you, Oliver Macdonald's unexpected defender. Good grief! The politics are a nightmare. So many peacocks. So many feathers to stroke. Anyway I'm sorry it has taken so long to get here. How are you? How are you coping?'

'I'm Brer Rabbit,' Will says brightly, 'in the briar patch.

These tunnels were my second home. Plus, being locked up has given me time to think. In between all the chatter from next door, that is.'

Tim Weston scoffs loudly.

Rani recognises his voice. Immediately she knows he outlived the trial and the coin toss. Letting go of Will's fingers, she bounds across to Tim's door, greets him warmly and tells him how wonderful it is that he made it through and has been reunited with Will, even though the circumstances of their reunion are less than ideal. All this she conveys with barely a word.

Returning to Will's door, she asks how Will is passing the time.

'I've been thinking.'

'About what?'

'Everything really. My parents' theories. Inlandia. The New Regime. The old Republic. How the world works. The past. The future. I've been going over everything I've seen, everything I've learnt – from my father and the Queen and Uncle Max and the Inlandians. What I've learnt from Laura, and my neighbour, and the Engine. And you, of course. I've learnt a great deal from you. The thing is, I think I've discovered something that makes sense of it all. Something that helps fit everything together. Soon I'll fill you in on where I've got to. First, though, Tim and I have a favour to ask. We were half expecting you, hoping you would come. Tim can tell you about his plans.'

Rani walks two paces back to Tim's door-hole.

'What is it?' she asks. 'And how can I help?'

'It's about Laura. I feel so bad for her. Just a single crummy coin-toss separated her father's fate from mine. I knew her a little. Met her a few times at Ashburnham High. Now I feel strangely bound to her. It's hard to explain but I feel I have to keep her safe. I think I can escape from here, and help her escape from Port Phillip. But first I need you to take a message to her. And a poem I wrote.'

The two prisoners had discussed Tim's plans at length. Will even suggested improvements to the poem. His former self – the Will before the Underworld and the Midwinter Debate – would've felt a tinge of jealousy: Tim had fallen for the same braided hair and squarish head that so enchanted Will in high school. Tim had carved Laura's name on Trajan's Column.

But that version of Will is long gone. Now, he only wants the best for Loopy Weston. And he vows to do everything he can to help. So does Rani, and Will feels no jealousy about that either.

After an affectionate farewell, Rani leaves with Tim's message and poem. She will find Laura and speak to her in secret. The poem, Tim hopes, will help convince Laura that he is genuine – he has, after all, poured his idiosyncratic heart into it. In the meantime he finalises his escape plans.

Will helps in the planning, even though his feelings about the escape are fiendishly conflicted. On the eve of the break-out, he confesses his feelings to his old friend.

'I have an urge to go with you,' he says, 'but also an urge to stay. I'm not sure what I'm going to do next, but I think I can do what I need to from here. I hope you don't think I'm a coward for not joining you. For not trying to get out.'

'There's definitely no cowardice in staying here. Just as there was no cowardice in Redcliffe. We've never spoken about this, but I never thought less of you for not riding the bommie. You were much younger than me. I shouldn't have pushed you. I'm sorry I did. And I'm sorry it hurt our friendship.'

In the end, escaping from the makeshift cell is a simple matter for the former janitor who learnt to fight on the dusty streets of Redcliffe, and who honed his skills in the back-blocks of Port Phillip and on the aqueducts of Inlandia.

Tim curls up in the corner of his cell. Will calls the guards over and tells them his silent neighbour must be ill. Rosencrantz and Guildenstern enter the cell warily and fully armed. As soon as Rosencrantz leans over to take a look at the inmate, Tim grabs him and clunks his head hard against the concrete wall.

In short order he knocks out Guildenstern as well, using Rosencrantz's halberd. Putting on Rosencrantz's uniform, he looks every bit a Spartan. Then, his madly grinning face appearing in Will's door-hole, he bids farewell and leaves to add a new chapter to his story.

# 39

# THE SHAPE OF THINGS

A FEW DAYS LATER, Rani visits Will for a second time. Concern and fear are obvious on her drained face and in her faltering voice.

'They got away,' she says, 'but they're in dreadful strife. The New Regime promised to disband the Actuaries but in fact it merely renamed them. They're now called the "Nostrato". They're active and on the loose with a new set of orders. And there's worse news than that. Lord Krull has installed himself as their leader. Tim and Laura set off along the old postal route that hugs the coast, then swings inland from Warrnambool all the way to Adelaide and Perth. I don't know how far they've got, but rumour has it that the assassins are already in pursuit. In hindsight it was a mad thing to do, to try to escape. This isn't Shakespeare or Austen. Tim and Laura aren't Romeo and Juliet. And they aren't young lovers running off to Gretna Green. This is real life. I've seen with my own eyes what the Nostrato are capable of. Tim and Laura are in grave danger, if they're not already dead. After the Inlandian takeover, there really is nowhere to hide.'

Will immediately shares Rani's worst fears. He misses Tim terribly. And Laura, too. After a few seconds he speaks.

'You're in danger as well. The New Regime might suspect you of helping our friends. Mad or not, I want you to go to Redcliffe. You'll be safer there, if it's possible to be safe anywhere.'

Rani considers this for a moment.

'I'll go there,' she says. 'If you think that's best. I trust you. What was it you wanted to tell me?'

'The key to all this. The upshot of Inlandia and our trek and my parents' search for truth. The solution to everything. At least I hope so. It could be the opposite. It could be the solution to nothing at all.'

'I know you well enough to know it's not that. You have to share it with me. Tell me what's on your mind and I'll tell you honestly what I think.'

Will steels himself, as though he's about to make a speech, or a confession. Then he lets loose, disgorging the private thoughts he has carefully organised in his cramped and roachy cell.

'Over the past months, I've seen and felt different realities. I've seen people and things transformed by nothing more than ideas and prejudices, expectations and beliefs. I have a new understanding of my parents' theories and their work. It's hard for me to say so, but I think they were both on the wrong track.

'My mother was right to challenge the Republican picture of central Australia as a null, a place of emptiness and silence. She was right to regard the published history of Australia as a fiction. But she and the other Inlandians also erred in the world they painted. They thought they were revealing the true history of Australia, but they were just obscuring it, even more than the Republic did. The Inlandians are as wrong about the past as they are about the future. They filled the emptiness in a counterfeit way with every kind of mad, centralian fantasy, knitted together into a kooky pastiche and a hotchpotch world view. Inlandia is a wrong turn. This whole Mkdoan reality is. And I'm sure there've been others. Wrong turns, that is. I'm also sure there was never any emptiness to fill in the first place. When the explorers came from across the seas, there was already a civilisation here – a civilisation without stilts or pyramids or perambulators but with its own complexity and richness. The Republic and Mkdos both painted on a canvas that wasn't blank. They covered up the ancient history of Australia, turning its people into bit-part players, and ghosts.

'And then there's my father. In searching for my mother he did his best to understand the world and to make sense of Inlandia and how it came to be. People, he believed, can marshal fundamental particles and strings into local realities. And the Mkdorii were able to do this on a spectacular scale – making a rich world that could persist because the Outlanders didn't believe in it.

'But he, too, was wrong. I don't think there ever were any strings or particles or dark matter. Or maybe they did exist, but only temporarily, as symptoms of more basic causes. The Teacher, for all his faults, knew this – that a deeper truth was at work behind the things we see and measure. And I think I know what that truth is. Scientists have reached the wrong conclusion from the double-slit experiment. The strange, contradictory, wave–particle nature of light isn't a contradiction between states of matter or energy. It's a contradiction between stories. So, too, my father's psychological experiments. He thought the Messiahs and Narcissists could dominate reality by being the most powerful observers. What he really detected, I think, is who was the best storyteller.

'I now believe the world, at the most primary level, is not a set of atoms or energies or chemical reactions. I believe webs of words and ideas are more fundamental. Think of our journey to Inlandia. We seemed to walk through one story after another. Our whole lives have been made up of stories

– of ambition and migration, danger and discovery, love and loss. And think of what we've learnt from the world's greatest thinkers and pioneers. People such as Darwin and Columbus and Galileo. Behind every physical truth, there's a great storyteller.

'Inlandia is further proof. The Teacher and de Rougemont and Buckley could co-create Inlandia by telling great stories. Remember Bruno? And the sea of rats? The clash between the Mkdorii and the Republic was a contest of stories.'

Rani gives Will a generous, curious look.

As Will continues, he is struck by how much he sounds like his father.

'I believe the world, and the whole universe for that matter, consists at the most basic level of stories. That's all there is, all there ever was. Stories – not particles or strings – are the truest truth. I don't mean this in a metaphorical "Never-ending Story" sort of way. I mean it in a real, physical sense. More real than any of Mandelbrot's metals and gasses and mixtures. The world wasn't shaped by observers acting on matter. It was shaped by storytellers adding to and adapting stories. The very first one must've sprung, fully formed, from pure nothingness. Straight out of the void. Maybe it was a simple tale of a serpent, or of attraction and repulsion, or of infinitesimal beings of thought and light. You can tell this is guesswork, I know, but humour me. As stories merged and grew and became more complex, the story-beings would've needed a world. And what is a world but a few simple things? A stable, navigable surface. The compass points. And the vertical directions – upwards to sun, moon and the canopy of stars, downward to earth and stone and, farther still, to fire. In that simple world, the story-beings would've made yet more stories. And as their stories were added to and changed, the world and the beings would've changed, too. Ever more intricate tales would've been told. About different types of beings – maybe they were recognisably people and animals by now. And about the insides of their bodies and how to make other living creatures. And about the large and small physics of the world, and the fabric of sky and space. Sometimes the stories were so changed in the telling that ironclad truths became obvious lies.'

Will thinks of Jenny and the unforgettably horrible moment when the monster finally enveloped her. Its oily mass intruded into the corners of her wide and terrified eyes, turning them to mercury.

'The continual remaking of the reality probably left behind a kind of cosmic frass: a detritus of false starts and junk realities and half-finished creations that infest our forgotten places, and our nightmares. The Minotaur in its Labyrinth. The Kraken at the Edge of the World. Even the Krampus and his basket of naughty children.'

Will pauses as he considers the history of writers and prophets and thinkers who've added to humankind's library of stories. He remembers Rani's stories from ancient India. The Teacher's stories from ancient Inlandia. Uncle Max's primordial tales of mortality and sin. And he considers all the lost stories of ancient Australia.

'The creation of ever newer stories changed the sun and the moon and the shape of the world. Take Copernicus. He told a convincing tale about how the world was a sphere. His story persuaded people and it became true. Scientists and doctors wrote of people as creatures of matter and chemistry, not of words or spirit or divine light. Those stories also stuck. Instead of luminous entities, we became mechanisms of flesh and organs and humours. The heart, such a poetic and storied organ, was thereafter just a pump. Science made a massive error. It misunderstood the place of people in the universe. For Copernicus and Galileo and their followers, the physical world was central. Humans were secondary, inconsequential to how everything worked. But I've seen how human belief and human authority are fundamental. How they can overcome any physical force. How they can *make* reality – and bend it, just as Mandelbrot showed matter could bend space-time. Mandelbrot himself, by the way, was one of the greatest storytellers who ever lived. Despite what the Theory and the Republic said, humans aren't inconsequential. We're not secondary or dispensable, a chemical smear. I think my father realised this after he reached Inlandia. I think he regretted swallowing the Republican line – and teaching it – about how small and accidental the earth is, and about how human timescales and human civilisations are just blips in an indifferent, unthinking eternity. People aren't irrelevant. We're not the scum of the universe. We're the centre. Human thoughts, human feelings, human deeds and human stories prevail over matter and all the physical forces. Each one of us is vastly more complex and potent than a hundred billion unpopulated galaxies.'

Rani ponders the strange vision that Will is painting. She imagines what the universe would look like from outside time and space. Powerful, existence-shaping ripples, propagating outward from prophets and theorists like waves in pan-dimensional water disturbed by pan-dimensional pebbles. Bubbles propagating threads of stories – about the cosmos, monsters, human flesh, the properties of the elements, the shape of the world. Words making waves. Words making worlds.

And she thinks of Tim and Laura. Maybe, in some sense, they really are Romeo and Juliet after all.

# 40

## THE TRUTHFUL OBSERVER

'THIS IS WHAT I KNOW,' Will says, exhausted. 'The problem is what to do about it. My mother was right about my being unimpressive. Despite genius parents, I was devastatingly average at school. I'm not the one to make a new reality. For one thing, I'm not sure what that reality should be. The Republicans and Inlandians both tried to overwrite the past. Surely others, too, had attempted to as well. But there's no such thing as a perfect world or a perfect society. There's much to like in what we have now – and much to regret – just as there was in the Republic. Who should get to say when the world needs to be redrafted?

'And even if I did meddle – if I tried to recast or replace the Mkdoan world – I'm not sure what would happen. We could all be killed. Or we could all be transformed, even more than we were changed by Inlandia's fountain of youth. Maybe we would just end up where we started. Anything's possible.'

Will thinks of John and Jenny, and of what he saw in the Underworld. He trembles at the memory of the creature from the abyss and its deadly appetite.

'Even the souls of the dead could return to the world. Or

they could be lost forever. I'm not the one to figure all this out. I'm not the one to make the new future.'

'I've seen your grades,' Rani says. 'Your whole file for that matter. Never forget that I'm your social worker! You've always been brainy. And always too hard on yourself. Ever ready to see the worst in what you did or didn't do, and to take criticism to heart. But this is your reality. You made it. You're the hero. Now *you* have to grab hold of it. Look at what you've done so far. Imagine what you *could* do.'

'Not much of a hero. *You're* the heroic one. Always so fearless, so driven, so confident. Nothing fazes you. Remember it was you who rescued me from Murnania. You who led the archers in the Battle for Inlandia. And it was Max who saved us from the Tannahill basement. Grig who rescued me from the Underworld. The Engine who saved me in the debate. And I . . . I couldn't save Jenny. I'm hopeless. Always in trouble, always afraid, imagining dangers all around, thinking people are spies. I even thought you were a spy, after Murnania.'

'I was half a spy,' Rani says. 'So was Jenny. And Tim, too. So you were half right, about being surrounded.'

Will thinks of all the people he and Rani have lost. Her parents and his father. Jenny, too, and most likely Tim and Laura – along with her marvellous globe. And he thinks of all the people who suffered in the Inlandian victory. And the thousands, perhaps millions of people – many of them unnamed and unknown – who perished in earlier purges and calamities, leaving behind such terrible silences.

'I'm not Adam and this world isn't mine. But I'll do as you say. I'll try to change things. I've thought of a way to unleash some powerful forces. Maybe the most powerful forces in the universe. I'm worried though. I don't want everything to go back to how it was before we found Inlandia. Most of all, I want you to be like this, always. A princess. And not . . . ,' Will hesitates, smiles. 'Not a boring, brown, bureaucrat.'

'I,' Rani says, 'was never boring.'

∞

Rani waits nervously outside Will's cell while he writes a letter and draws a map on a piece of Rani's notepaper. In the letter, which is addressed to Maximillian Bunt, Will thanks his father's uncle for the backpack and the pistol and the knife. And he apologises for leaving him behind after Alan Smith's visit.

He reminds Max who Rani is – one of the two officials who called at his house in Redcliffe – and he hints that he and Rani have been through much together, and have formed a partnership – one that Max would understand and approve of. Finally, at the end of the letter, he asks Max to embark on a mission. A perilous mission, and almost certainly a hopeless one.

When Will is finished he hands the note to Rani through the door-hole. She quickly grabs his fingers and holds them to her cheek, before kissing them.

'I hope,' she says, 'this is not our final goodbye.'

Will is sad and frightened and delighted all at once. He utters no words in response but his eyes say everything.

Rani goes straight to her apartment, packs some essential things, then sets off for Redcliffe. In her former life as a low-ranking official, she sometimes transited between Redcliffe and the capital. Now, the transport system has been transformed but she still knows how to travel efficiently and with a low profile. She makes it to Redcliffe safely and is soon sitting on Uncle Max's sofa.

'Would you like some lemon butter bread?' Max asks. 'And some Earl Grey?'

The bachelor disappears into the kitchen. Rani scans the room, which is lined with cabinets and shelves heavy with porcelain. She thinks of Will living in this house. All the rules, all the fragile ceramics. He must've been permanently on eggshells.

A few minutes later, Max returns with the bread and the tea.

'Now,' he says, 'let's get down to business.'

'Will's drawn a map. You'll have to get past a Spartan guard or two.'

'Easily done,' Max says. 'When people reach a certain age, my dear, they become utterly invisible. The assassins aren't the only masters of stealth.'

# 41

## THE PERFECT FORM

ARMED WITH WILL'S map and instructions, Max embarks on a not-very-fast race against time.

He travels by airship to Port Philip's blimp-port, then by steam-driven charabanc to Sandstone. Passing two sets of guards effortlessly, he finds the starting point marked on the map. Opening the trap door, he climbs awkwardly and snugly into the tunnel beneath Cromwell's Cloister.

No one in the world knows better than Will how to navigate from the South Tower to the Northern Lawn, or from the Law Lounge to the Union Building, or from the Cloister to the loading dock, without being seen.

'Thank goodness for Will,' Max thinks to himself. 'And for pilates.'

He quickly finds his bearings in the tunnels and is soon brushing away cobwebs on the approach to the heavy oak door. A small mercy: the door is still ajar. No-one has come this way since Will and Loopy's panicked flight.

Max squeezes through the gap into the vestibule, then climbs the steep flight of stairs. At the ancient stone wall he feels around for the raised block, finds it, gives it a push, hears it click, watches the gateway swing open, then squeezes himself through the secret entrance to the Chamber of Logic.

Inside the Chamber there is no movement and no noise apart from the low hum and metallic whirr of the Consistency Engine.

The Engine is shaped like a giant sleeping lion. Having been worn out by Lord Krull's fumbling attempts to make it de-sphere the world, it is taking a rest.

After the Inlandian victory, the Engine's computer interface went on the fritz, as did the back-up, the old punch-card system. Sandstone's engineers jerry-rigged a new mechanical interface but Max ignores that. He will address the Engine directly.

With neither reverence nor fear, Maximillian Bunt, collector of porcelain and of stories, walks right up to the Engine and begins to speak. First, he reads from a short script that Will scribbled at the bottom of his note. Then he shares the biblical stories of Genesis, the Flood and the Resurrection. Much older stories, too, of fire and wind and ice; and of animal spirits and earth magic.

And then he improvises, confiding in the Engine his opinions and superstitions. The goings on in Redcliffe. Which of his neighbours make the best cakes and grow the best flowers. And who did what to whom in his extended family, going back four generations.

In a formless monologue that sounds like the unrhymed verse of an experimental poet – and a provincial, geriatric one at that – Max lays out his theories of life and fate and the universe. How there's more to the world than what we can see and measure. How everything has a purpose, and life is a kind of test.

The Engine listens attentively to the soliloquy, trying to digest the rapid flow of words. As every idea penetrates into its machine-mind, the Engine adopts a physical form that represents the word-picture. The result is spectacular. No-one has ever seen anything like it before.

Looking like a contortionist who is playing Twister and charades at the same time – and who drank too much coffee beforehand – the Engine moves faster and faster, forming itself into shape after shape.

In the twisting flurry of mechanical movement, a diligent observer might've noticed three-dimensional representations of hats and teapots, shoes and ladders, cats and pentagrams, even an old man with his prize-winning pound-cakes and azaleas.

As the Engine tries harder and harder to keep up, its joints strain and its cogs steam. The floor begins to vibrate alarmingly and a noise like a jet plane at full power fills the Chamber. Uncle Max has to shout louder and louder to be heard.

And then the whizzing, burning, screaming Engine settles on the perfect form with which to represent Max's words. Entertaining a hundred inconsistent theories at once, the Engine takes the shape of a thousand inconsistent thoughts. And the only way to do so is to explode into a hundred thousand sparkling smithereens.

The explosion sends forth in every direction an extraordinary pulse of reality-transforming energy. The strangest, most powerful wave ever to be let loose in all the history of time. Racing, churning, consuming. The pulse overwhelms everything in its path. Everything is vacuumed up into nothingness.

The end of the Engine, therefore, is the end, too, of the Chamber of Logic. And of all the other buildings at Sandstone. And of all of Port Phillip. And of every other object and organism in the known universe.

Will Page, alone and lonely in the temporary dungeon below Sandstone, is one of the first organisms to be gobbled up by the vacuuming wave. Standing right next to the seat of the surge, Maximillian Bunt disappears even sooner.

A brief instant before Max is consumed, the diligent observer would've noticed on his face a serene expression of infinite accomplishment.

**42**

----

**BEACH**

IN A UNIVERSE of absolute nullifying annihilation, nothing happens. Nothing *can* happen. Dark, silent, empty oblivion stretches to infinity in every direction and every dimension. In all space and no space. For all time and no time.

No, not for all time. After a long pause, the nothingness bulges and stretches, then bends and cracks. Through folds and fractures in the empty universe a little miracle breaks into the darkness, just as it did once before. The miracle creates a tiny patch of story in the void.

Faint little story-motes pop into and out of existence, like random notes of music, or the flirting, flitting, fleeting lights of fireflies. Then one of the motes brightens. Will Page's min-min. His guardian angel. His story.

Soon another of the lights breaks away from the flickering motes and begins to move purposefully towards Will's story. The second light pulses radiantly as though it is pleased. Or amused.

'What is this place?' Will's story asks.

'I've been here before,' the other light says. 'I'm starting to remember. I think it's called the netherworld. Or heaven.

You can call it what you like. The name of the place doesn't matter, just as my name doesn't.'

'The dead come here, don't they? I mean souls, like me.'

'Yes. And the souls of animals. Other beings, too. You don't think all that effort to create a living creature just goes to waste, do you? Disappears like it meant nothing? No. That wouldn't make any sense.'

'Are there bad things in the darkness? Are there monsters? Is this a good place?'

'So many questions! As places go, I suppose it is. But it isn't perfect. There are dangers in every place.'

Will's story considers this for a long moment.

'It's a kind of refuge, then. A kind of paradise.'

'You were always the optimist. Always looking on the bright side. To me it's simply home. I lived here from when time began. From when the great serpent swept across the skies. But for you, my friend, it's time to go.'

∞

Up and down. Land and sea. Day and night. Sun and moon.

Will and Rani.

It takes a while for them to orient themselves and to remember who they were and what they'd done before the remaking of the world.

The person who'd been Will Page is first to remember himself. The feeling is like waking up and half recalling a vivid dream.

Then the person who'd dreamt of Rani realises that she is Rani's dream, and that she has also been, all along, Rani herself.

Standing on the warm, white sand of a beautiful ocean beach, Will and Rani embrace. Then they kiss.

Eventually Rani asks a question, for the sake of saying something.

'Have you seen this beach before?'

Will hasn't. He answers with a bit of irrelevant history.

'The first part of Australia to appear on a map was called Beach.'

The sun prepares to set in the west. The uppermost clouds turn from grey-pink to dark purple with patches of red. As the dusk deepens, the stars begin to come out.

Will and Rani take in their surroundings. Everything feels calm, safe, perfect.

Though the sun is going down, the air is still warm. The stars – and the moon – provide ample light.

Rani feels an urge to explore. As she walks off along the beach, Will watches her go. When he can't see her anymore he sits down, stretches out his legs, scrunches his toes in the sand and watches the breakers roll in. He imagines what it would be like to surf their glassy, tubular perfection.

After half an hour Rani comes bounding back along the beach.

'I saw people,' she says, panting, momentarily breathless. 'Past the rocky point. You have to come.'

'What people? Who did you see?'

Rani pauses, catches her breath, savours the moment. Then she smiles beautifully, joyfully.

'Everyone.'

www.ingramcontent.com/pod-product-compliance
Lightning Source LLC
Chambersburg PA
CBHW020138120726
47903CB00007B/2308